Forgotten Past

A Novel
by

Jacqueline Opresnik

ISBN 978-1-7774328-5-0 e-book
ISBN 978-1-777-4328-6-7 book

Cover Design by Sandra Muzyka

For Jack,
who would have
understood how Alice felt.

Other Books

by

Jacqueline Opresnik

The Misha Plate

How to Make Money Flowers

Package from the Past

In Search of Jeremy Griffin

The Grants of Maxwell Street

The Grants at War

The Hunt for William Williamson

Murder in the Asylum

Forgotten Past

Chapter 1

2022 Niagara, Ontario, Canada

The house was smaller than she had imagined, considering the neighbour-hood; a one-story, ranch-style home on a large treed lot. Perhaps it was because the home was dwarfed on either side by massive modern two-storey buildings, homes of a newer, richer population having settled in this peaceful community.

She did wonder about her new client, though. What would compel an elderly eighty-four-year-old woman to suddenly want to know about her family's genealogy?

Meg slowed down her car and pulled into the gated driveway, the gates having been left open to accommodate her visit. She took a final look in the mirror, tidying her hair before opening the door. This was her third commission since starting her own genealogy business a little over a month ago, and it didn't hurt to make a good impression.

She'd parked under a large tulip tree and gathered her folders before getting out and approaching the door. A few drops of rain fell from the branches above, left over from the early morning shower. The grey sky had given over to white fluffy clouds and now promised a warm summer day, humid; this close to the lake.

The home itself was covered with various grays of natural stone, whether solid stone or sheets of a modern replica, Meg couldn't tell. A large medieval-looking door dominated the entrance, with a larger metal door-knocker in the centre just below a wrought iron-covered, peek-window. The wooden door opened before she had a chance to rap with the knocker, and a young man smiled invitingly. She wondered who he might be then the thought disappeared as he spoke.

"You must be Meg Fletcher," he said. The handsome young man was tall and dressed casually in jeans and blue denim shirt. "I'm Flynn Williams." She smiled and was rewarded with a smile that extended to his hazel eyes. He opened the door further, and stood back, inviting her in. "Gran is waiting for you in the living room."

The foyer gave a homey smell of wood and lemon polish, as the dark walnut paneling extended into the living area. Alice Williams sat on a large velvet green chair. Her smile warm, her eyes, possibly hopeful.

Flynn showed her to an arranged chair opposite, while he took up the arm of the large chair, close to his grandmother.

"I suppose you're wondering why I suddenly want to learn about my family now, at my age?" Alice gave her a rueful smile. She seemed to be a small woman, but not frail. Her hair wasn't white but a salt and pepper gray, rather straight, in a short-style haircut. "Like most young people in the fifties and sixties I was consumed by my own life," she began. "Things were not easy after the war. There was a recession in the fifties. By the mid sixties I was married, with my baby boy, and worked part time. I was left a widow in ninety-three when my husband, Richard, died of a burst appendix."

She patted the hand of her grandson, and smiled. "When Flynn's father asked me recently about my parents, it occurred to me how little I actually knew … about my history. I'd like him to know his roots and pass that on to his two children."

Flynn gave his grandmother a hug with his free arm. "I'm afraid I was just as guilty with my own life to even think about asking about my father's grandparents," he added.

Meg smiled at their joined enthusiasm. "Well, I'm confident we can fill in a lot of the blanks for you," she said, then opened up her folder ready to take pertinent notes and to share the plan she proposed to use.

"Of course, you know your parents' names, but not your mother's maiden name; you said over the phone. Do you know anything else about your parents that might be a place to start?"

"My father had been a soldier during the war. He had a great many health issues after he returned in 1945. My mother always thought they were due to the night he spent in a freezing river in France behind enemy lines, hiding from the Germans with two of his men. He was captured the next morning after the body of one of the soldiers who died during the night, was seen by a passing patrol. He was taken to the Gestapo headquarters in the area the next day and interrogated."

"My father never spoke of his war experiences to me; I guess I was too young or maybe it was too painful to relive what had happened to him, but my mother always thought the Nazis had beat him, broke his leg and fractured his ribs during their interrogation. He was sent to a prisoner of war camp after that, where a British doctor cared for him. He stayed there until the end of the war."

"He had arthritis bad and a limp when he walked," she added. A look of sadness came over her face. "He died in 1966, a week after I married. I always thought he had waited, hung on to life, until he knew I'd be taken care of. He liked Richard and knew he was a good man. On his death bed he asked Richard to look after my mother as well, which he did until she died."

"My mother never spoke of my father after that and there were only a few friends at the funeral, no family." Her eyes were saddened and her face took on a questioning look. "I often wondered why I had no grandparents, or aunts or uncles that came to visit us ... all those years, but not enough I guess to question it."

She gave Meg a sad smile acknowledging her lack of interest then. "I wish I had asked more questions. But you know how it is with young people, usually wrapped up with their own existence; school and social connections."

Mother died the year after my father; from a broken heart I always thought, although the doctors said it was a brain aneurysm."

Meg nodded in understanding. She understood well, the loneliness that came with losing a parent. Her own father had died while on a fishing trip when she was twelve. But in Alice's case not having any other family for support must have been very difficult.

"Not having any family on one parent's side due to perhaps a falling out, happens, but having no one on both sides is a bit unusual," she said. "So, I would suggest we also do a DNA test." She smiled encouragingly. "You may have family out there."

That got the encouraging smile she was hoping for. Perhaps Alice hadn't been alone in the world, although if that were the case why hadn't relatives made themselves known when she was a child?

"There's one I like, that can go back fifty generations. They show you where your ancestors are from, and when they entered your family. But unfortunately for us, that one is private and while it might help greatly with a family tree, it wouldn't let you know if you had extended family members. There is another one that gives you ... some people say a vague family pie-graph representing the areas of the world your family comes from ... but they are a public source of DNA genealogical results that link people together, that is, if they've also taken that same test, so I would suggest a site that has public results and is quite prolific in their data."

5

Alice looked at her grandson for his approval. "Is that all right, do you think?"

He smiled at her hesitancy wondering if she had second thoughts. "I think it should be fine, Gran. I can't really think of a negative."

"I would suggest we use this one, then," Meg pointed to one of five on her sheet she had listed, "because you're more likely to discover"—she considered her client's advanced age— "cousins from their site, and from there we can expand back into previous generations."

Alice gave her grandson a soft smile, and took his hand in hers. "I'm looking forward to this," she said. "It would be nice to know where I came from, who my people were, and possibly have some connection."

Meg leaned forward and gave her free hand a gently pat. It wasn't hard to imagine how alone Alice must have felt growing up. She had a small family circle now and it was clear that her grandchildren meant a lot to her as well. "I'm sure we will be able to find some answers for you."

Alice looked at Meg as if she suddenly thought of something. "Forgive my manners, would you care for a coffee or tea, or something cool?"

"If you'll join me, yes, thank you."

"I'll take care of that, Gran. What about ice tea?"

Alice nodded. "That would be fine, Flynn. I think Martha made a fresh batch this morning."

Flynn was only gone a few minutes and returned with a tray of glasses and a pitcher of iced tea, already frosted with condensation from the warm day. He poured a glass for each of them then resumed his previous place next to his grandmother.

After a sip of his cool drink, he put his glass down on the tray again, and looked at Meg, his eyes sparkling with the sudden eagerness of an idea that had just come to him.

"Why don't you come here to work. Now that we are talking about family genealogies, I'm thinking, while I have some time, that I could work on my mother's family while you work on my father's side for Gran."

Meg held her glass, cool against her hand and considered this. Flynn was definitely enthusiastic and although she thought it might be counter-productive to work with a client, she considered the alternative.

Having lived in her home for only three days now, at the moment her new office was in her living room and consisted of a filing cabinet, one wooden folding table, and a computer still packed away in its box with her printer, along with the living rooms customary furnishings of couch, chair and coffee table.

Having a larger space to work in and enough table space to lay out the findings would be welcome. She would probably have to guide this budding genealogist in his hunt, but on second thought that might be interesting. She'd felt the attraction when he had first opened the door for her and now ...

"I think, I will take you up on your offer," she said, and was rewarded with a nod and a smile. "What time should I be here tomorrow?"

He hadn't expected that, and thought for a moment considering. "How is one o'clock?"

"Fine, I'll see you both then." They finished their drinks at leisure, after which Flynn walked her to the door.

He stood at the entrance and watched as she drove away.

"Well, that was interesting," said Alice. She had joined him at the door to wave goodbye. "I didn't think you were that interested in your family history." Then she gave her grandson a knowing look. "I assume you find her interesting, or should I say attractive?"

Flynn returned the look then smiled. "Well, I might. I won't know yet, the interesting part I mean." His face betrayed his thought and he smiled at his grandmother. "Besides, it might be fun to look up my Mum's side of the family, especially if I'm sitting next to a beautiful brunette."

His grandmother gave a small snort at that. "Well, you might be able to fake an interest in genealogy but how are you going to conjure up an office in this house by tomorrow."

"There's only one room, I can think of that might be all right." He gave his grandmother an expectant look. "The library?"

Alice contemplated this, enjoying his discomfort. "Perhaps. Of course, you'll have to move the furniture. There is a long table in the basement you could use."

His hope of pulling off this deception now part-way realized, he added, "I can bring my computer and laptop from home and a printer." Then a panicked look came over him. "You do have the internet here, don't you?"

This made his grandmother laugh. "I don't use a computer you know that, but yes. Your sister had it installed last year after she bought me a SMART T.V. for my birthday."

"Oh, thank goodness. I better hurry, I'll need a couple of friends to help move furniture around. Then I'll have to go to the store and buy a few things." He leaned over and gave his grandmother a kiss on the cheek. "Thanks, Gran." Then bounded out the front door, car keys in hand, leaving his grandmother amazed at his exuberance.

Chapter 2

The afternoon was bright and warm, and Meg was looking forward to her first day researching Alice's family. Traffic was hectic in the town as tourists and shoppers randomly crossed the main street in search of bargains. Cars gave way creating a slow progression into town. She hoped the office space would be conducive to working and not a small cramped room. After a night of restless sleep, she was at least honest enough with herself to know that she was looking forward to working with Flynn too.

There was something about him she liked besides his looks; maybe his energy or perhaps his concern for his grandmother.

Meg was warmly greeted by the family as she left her car, and escorted by Flynn through the room they had sat in the day before to the office room. It wasn't exactly what she had envisioned by the word 'office'. It would have made a lovely library in itself; the walls lined with shelving, held books from top to bottom. There was a large fireplace on the wall opposite large double-paned windows that now let in the early afternoon light from the back yard.

A wooden table, that appeared in a previous life to be a dining room table, big enough to sit eight comfortably, stood in the centre of the room. Office supplies took up space at one end, while the electronics they would be working on stood waiting at the opposite end.

Two chairs that were definitely not part of the original suite sat side by side on their roller feet. Flynn watched her reaction to his handiwork and was rewarded with a nod of approval. "This should work well," she said and sat her computer case and notepads on the table.

Meg set her laptop at one of the stations indicated by the chair placement and plugged her cord into the power bar below the table. She smiled to herself as she noticed how rather than taking up any other space along the wooden table, Flynn had placed his working station along side hers.

She'd thought about the proposal more, once while she was at home, although the thought of working with Flynn was both intriguing and questionable, especially given the grandmother's reaction to his declared interest in his mother's history.

Having to guide a person unfamiliar with research while also doing her own work might prove draining and involve excess time. At the same time, though, he was charming and eager and she was curious where such a collaboration might lead.

"I'm glad you decided to work here," said Flynn.

"Actually, so am I. I've only been in my new house a few days and still have a large bin in my driveway to unload. My office wasn't exactly my priority."

He smiled at that, pleased she found his makeshift working area suitable. "I'm off for a while, if you find you need any help."

"Thank you." She considered his offer and decided to take him up on his proposal. "I could use a bit of help. Are you free tomorrow morning?"

He smiled, hoping he'd get an invite to help her. "At your service, nine o'clock?"

"That would be great."

They took their places, ready to begin.

His hands were poised over the computer keyboard in anticipation of all the great finds he would make this day. He smiled at her, wondering if she was suitably impressed. "Where do we start?" he asked.

"It's not quite that easy. I doubt you will find much of your mother's family today."

Before he could ask why, she elaborated, "... because your immediate family is too recent for there to be a great deal of information that's not covered by privacy laws."

He leaned back giving her a questioning look. "What if my mother is Scottish?" he said, not quite sure if that would improve the hunt or not.

"That makes a small difference." Then she laughed. "There are some steps you need to take before you start. What you need to do first is speak to your mother and see how much information you can get about grandparents and great grandparents etc., then make a family chart for her family."

She leaned over and began outlining the shape of his chart on the large writing pad provided, starting with his mother Mary Flynn, then left spaces for each generation. "When you've found out all you can, then you can start with the genealogy sites. He gave her a deflated look as if he was being given a massive amount of math problems to work on before being allowed to go out for recess.

"Oh, and be sure to get dates and locations for each generation regarding births, marriages and deaths, even if it's only approximate."

He leaned back in his chair, disappointed at not being able to work beside her for the near future. "Well, I'd better start then. My mother should be home." He pushed his chair back, the rolling feet gliding easily on the wooden floor.

He picked up the notepad and wondered how she could begin with the information his grandmother had given her. "Where will you start?" he asked.

"Ah. Your grandmother knows her mother and father were both born in Ontario, and she knows her grandmother's first name was Lillian, but I'm afraid little more other than when they died."

So, I will begin by looking for a marriage certificate for Alice's parents sometime in the 1930s, hopefully before the privacy laws kicked in. That should give me their ages, and their parents' names and possibly her mother's maiden name, if not, then I will search for the parents' marriages to get her mother's maiden name and hence the names of their parents. Then I will look at the

13

census records. There are also city directories and newspapers that might hold some information."

"But before all that, I'll order the DNA test for Alice. It shouldn't take long to arrive, but a bit longer to analyze once she has prepared the sample."

Looking a bit more impressed by the enormity of her task, he smiled as Meg handed him a pen. "See you later, then."

Meg turned her computer on and waited as it warmed up, a smile forming on her face. The sun had moved around to the garden side of the house, enough now to catch the edge of the bevels of the garden windows. She was distracted by the flickering lights on the table top, and watched while the colours danced across the table as tree branches moved, causing the light to flicker through the leaves. She thought French doors would look nice on that wall, and wondered why no one had thought to create an entrance to the back yard from here.

A melodious tone signaled her machine was ready and she clicked on her favourite genealogy site, hoping she might get lucky in finding the marriage of Steven and Anne Hughes on her first go. After logging in, Meg plugged in the name of the groom and the first name of the bride, their birth dates, and location. She used Ontario for location which she thought would give her a wider sampling, just in case they weren't married in Toronto. It didn't take long for the search results to come back, because there were zero results matching her request. That was odd.

She revised her search and expanded the ages to plus or minus five years. Again, nothing. That was unusual but not unheard of. Perhaps the names had been misspelled or entered incorrectly. After numerous attempts she tried just using first names of the wedded couple, to see if any of the results came up In Ontario. There were two results, but when she checked the information, the dates and ages of the two couples were way off. She made a note of them in her notebook just in case.

With marriage information a 'no go', she decided to work backwards with the information she did know, so starting with 1965 she checked the names of the couple in the Toronto directory. There they were as Alice had said, living on Arundel Drive in Vaughn. She made note of her finding and continued back one year at a time until she got to 1945. Anne was still living at the same address but the directory showed no husband. Of course not, her husband was—according to his daughter Alice— currently a prisoner of war. So, after checking the war years for Anne and her address, Meg went further back to 1940 and again had success in finding the family home.

But 1939 was a surprise. There was no trace of Anne Hughes in Toronto. She checked further by considering all Ontario, and nothing. Where had the family gone?

Then she tried a different path. Alice Hughes was born in 1938. There should be a record, and that record should confirm her parents' names and address. There were records but not after 1917 due to privacy. The only birth information available for the 1930s that she found were only included in death records. But that was irrelevant, as the name Alice Hughes never came up for births in Ontario at all. That was strange.

"Will ye be staying for supper, Miss?" A diminutive woman, who looked older than Alice herself stood at the door.

"Well, I ..."

"Of course, she is," interrupted a male voice from the hall way. "You will, won't you?"

She still had research she'd like to work on today, and thought of the alternative;
sitting in a crowded living room surrounded by boxes that needed to be unpacked. "Yes, thank you. I'd like that."

"Good. Please make supper for three then, Martha."

Flynn pulled up his chair to the table, close to her, and glanced at her screen. "How's it going?"

Meg shook her head slowly. "Not as I would have hoped. There is no record of their marriage so far. I did find what your grandmother told us already about his death, in 'The Canada Find a Grave Index'. It did give birth year and birth place and I was hopeful, but when I looked further, no record came up for him, nothing, not even an obituary."

She shook her head slightly. "It's as if he didn't exist before 1940."

"That seems a bit strange. Is that usual?"
"No."

1939 Niagara Falls, Ontario

"All quiet corporal?"

"Yes, Sir." The soldier shook the rain slicker that covered his uniform, scattering the drops of mist that had gathered as water droplets, from the rubberized surface. "A bit wet though." He looked at the massive falls behind him, the cloud of mist hovering over the area above.

"Do you think this is necessary, sir. The patrol I mean."

Lieutenant Carter looked around at the area they were defending. "You remember the spy ring scare at Grand Bend last month; thousands of gallons of gasoline ready for German planes, with large quantities of dynamite and ammunition found. Even though there was no truth to it, people were scared. As to the Falls and our power station, I can't think of an easier target for terrorists, unless it's the Welland Canal." He gave the corporal an appraising look, then smiled. "It's reassuring for us to be here, corporal. Shows the population we are taking sabotage seriously. So, *you*, take it seriously and look as though you are defending the country. Yes?"

"Yes, sir!"

"I'll change you with Fenwick in another hour." The corporal saluted as the lieutenant took his leave to check on the next position up the walkway on the Niagara Parkway.

Lieutenant Carter walked up to the next checkpoint, mist from the falls hitting his face as he walked. He stopped when he reached the next station. Fenwick was no where to be seen. There was a shop near by that would have seen the soldier through their wide windows. Maybe the private had gone in. He could see the girl at the desk glance at him as he passed the window and entered the shop. It was a busy day apparently, having several other customers in the room.

"Have you noticed what happened to the soldier that was posted outside, Miss?" he asked. She was very young and if anyone would have noticed the handsome private, it would be her.

She glanced through the window as if expecting the soldier to suddenly appear. "He was there ten minutes ago, sir. He was talking to a man and then I had a customer to wait on and when I came back to the till he seemed to have moved away from the window."

"Thank you, Miss."

Lieutenant Carter went back outside and stood in the last place he remembered talking to Fenwick. He looked up and down the road and where the table rock looked out over the Canadian Horseshoe Falls. More tourists had arrived now as a shuttle bus unloaded the eager photographers. Everyone wanted a view of the falls.

A woman screamed and he turned abruptly in the direction of her distress. "A man is down there!" someone yelled. Two young men from the crowd jumped the stone wall and were making their way carefully down the rocky slope as he arrived and looked over the edge.

Fenwick. Lying awkwardly on the stones, blood discolouring his uniform along his side, his legs bent, dangerously close to the rushing waters of the river. Obviously, his attacker had intended for him to fall into the river and end up being swept away over the falls.

The crowd was swarming around the rescued man as the two young men helped him over the wide, red, sandstone wall.

Carter reached his Private and motioned the people back. He directed a man closest to him to go into the shop he had just left and call for the police and an ambulance. One of the young men was a fireman in everyday life and took steps to staunch the bleeding, as Carter questioned Fenwick.

"Two men," Fenwick gasped, "they carried rucksacks." He groaned with the pain, from a knife wound to the side. He grabbed Carter's sleeve and hung on, desperate to get the words out. "Explosives. Power station." Then he passed out.

"Look after him until the ambulance comes!" he said to Fenwick's rescuers. Then he took the fireman—who had heard what Fenwick had said—aside, and told him to send the police after him. The man nodded, understanding.

He turned back to the main road and looked south, towards the power station, then ran. He saw them. Carrying what he supposed were explosives. He threw off his own rain slicker making it easier to run. The sidewalk was slick with mist and he slipped. He had to catch up to them. People were walking towards him eager to see the falls and unaware of the danger that the two men proposed behind them.

He unsnapped the closure of his holster preparing to remove his revolver. No. He couldn't take the chance. Would a stray bullet hitting the bundles they carried on their backs ignite the explosives? He wasn't sure, but knew he couldn't take the chance.

He heard the distant wail of a siren and his mind eased somewhat at having left Fenwick. The crowd thinned as he walked on.

He saw the two men and they apparently saw him too, as they suddenly upped their pace.

A park police officer on a motorized cart pulled up next to him after being flagged down. "Something wrong, Lieutenant?"

He nodded to the officer, noticing that he was armed as he was with a revolver. "Saboteurs, come with me."

Together they drove up to the building, the two men having disappeared. Lieutenant Carter tapped the police officer's arm, and signaled him to stop. "You go that way," he said, motioning towards the front of the building, "and I'll go behind."

"They're carrying explosives and they've already tried to kill one man," he warned, "Shoot to kill, but be careful of the rucksacks they're carrying."

Chapter 3

2022 Niagara, Ontario, Canada

Supper was wonderful. Whether it was the delicious roast beef and roasted potatoes or the fact that she didn't have to make it herself, she couldn't say, either way she was appreciative.

"Martha is a fantastic cook," she said, meaning it. "Thank you for inviting me."

Alice smiled at the compliment. "She is. Martha's been with me since 1970."

Flynn sat across from her and smiled at the look on her face when Martha brought in a trifle for dessert. "We can go for a walk down by the lake if you'd like, after," he said, "to walk off our supper."

Alice ate little, but seemed to enjoy watching the young people at her table. "How have you made out today, with your search?" she asked.

"Not as well as I had hoped," Meg admitted. Then she added the disturbing fact that her parents didn't seem to exist prior to 1940.

Alice's face took on a look of disbelief, then one of concern, her brows creased in concentration. "How can that be? I'm here, and I was born in 1938, so they must have been somewhere in Ontario."

"I'm sure they were. Do you happen to have your birth certificate?" asked Meg, hopeful that a certificate would solve some questions. It might tell us where they were in 1938."

Alice hesitated before answering, "I … um, no. Mother would have had all of the required documents, and when she died, well, I never thought to look for them, and I don't remember coming across any papers that seemed important."

Meg could see a glimpse of distress in her client's face. She smiled. "Don't worry, we will figure it out."

"Yes, Gran. Meg and I will work on it after we have our walk."

Flynn gave Alice a reassuring smile which eased her own doubts a little. "Then, the sooner we start our walk the sooner we can continue looking," she said.

They walked down the road to the main street of the town, then crossed over and continued along the road on the other side towards the lake.

"It's been years since I've been here," she said. "When I was little, we used to come and visit my grandmother at her retirement home, then bring her here for a day of shopping." She looked around at the shops nearest them. "A lot has changed since then. There used to be a store on the corner that carried Canadian items, many made by our indigenous people. I usually bought a pair of moccasins that I kept for indoor use."

"You're right, a lot of things have changed, I remember that store too."

They walked until they came to a road that followed the contours of the lake. "It's a clear day, you can see Fort Niagara from here," Flynn said.

The lake was calm. A large freighter could be seen at a distance, ready for it's turn to enter the Welland Canal a few miles away.

He took her hand as they crossed the road and walked on to a grassy park area. She felt the warmth and electricity of his touch on her. "This means a lot to Gran," he said. "Finding her family, I mean. Do you think we can do it?"

She released her hand, and smiled, hoping to give some encouragement. "We?"

"Well, yes, surely I can help in some way."

There were a lot of documents that might help her find Alice's family and having another pair of eyes to help scan search results would indeed be of a help. "Yes, you can, and I would welcome your help."

"Good then, let's walk down to the edge of the lake." There was a man fishing along the shore and they waved as they went by.

Meg enjoyed the walk and surprisingly was enjoying her time talking to Flynn. He was a very enthusiastic, positive person, and obviously was able to pick up on her worried demeanour at what she had found so far.

There was a park bench on the edge of the grassy area overlooking the lake.

"Let's sit for a while," he suggested. "Then you can tell me what's bothering you."

Meg joined him on the bench and shook her head slowly. Now that she had an ally in this, perhaps she should discuss it and hopefully gain another perspective.

"I found the family on the Toronto directory for 1960 and followed them back to 1940, but before that, as I told you, it's as if they didn't exist. No marriage, no birth records, no electoral records or census records."

"What? That doesn't seem possible." Flynn didn't know much about records and what was available but this didn't sound right. "Why would that be?"

"The way I see it," she said, "is, one—the family was in another part of Canada prior to 1940 or out of the country altogether, and came to the area in 1940. If they went to the United States for few years prior to 1940, that might be difficult to trace, but it's a possibility. Or two—they were in Ontario under a different name. Anne lived in the same house as Alice grew up in during the war years, but not in 1939, or earlier.

"Why would a family change their name?" asked Flynn, suddenly more interested in his family records than he thought he would ever be.

"Many reasons," said Meg. "The least of which would be they just didn't like the name they had." Then she laughed at the thought, and dismissed the idea.

"Maybe my great grandfather was a criminal, maybe he committed bigamy and had to get out of town, or maybe he owed money to a loan shark and couldn't pay up," offered Flynn.

Meg laughed at his last suggestion. "Something must have happened before 1940, but what?"

"The war?" he offered. "Maybe he changed his name to avoid the army. Did Canada have the draft back then?"

"Somewhat. In 1940, they decided to have a national registration of eligible men and authorized conscription for home defence. It wasn't until 1944 that overseas duty was enforced."

Meg had been thinking along a similar line of thought. Britain had declared war on Germany, September 3, 1939. Canada had followed shortly after, joining the allies in September 10, 1939. "Let's look into the newspapers for 1938 and 1939 years, and see if something happened in Ontario that might explain …" She raised her hands, meant to encompass all possibilities.

Their walk cut short by their eagerness to start looking for this elusive family, Meg and Flynn went straight to the office area. Alice had gone to lay down for a while, siting a headache, and Meg felt partly responsible for upsetting the elderly woman.

Meg sat at her station while Flynn pulled up his chair next to her. "Where do we start?" he asked, eager to be of help as well as getting a chance to work with Meg.

"I'm also thinking we should check the passenger lists coming into Canada, as well as the newspapers."

"That sounds logical, considering I can't see why a family should change their name," reasoned Flynn. "So, which do I tackle, the newspapers, or the passenger lists?"

"Start with the passenger lists. Here, go onto this site. This is my username and password. Start by entering Steven Hughes and his birthdate 1915, give or take five years, then search under passenger lists and see what you can find. Make note of all of them, even if the age and location seem off."

They worked in companionable silence for the next hour, Flynn scanning page after page of search results, while Meg checked again for the family in other parts of Canada without success.

The wall clock struck seven-thirty as Meg started with the largest Toronto newspaper for the year 1939, starting in January and worked her way through the year. It was August of that year when she came upon an interesting story about saboteurs in Grand Bend, Ontario. The R.C.M.P. had debunked the rumours of Nazi planes, stored ammunition and potential threats, but local gossip continued with uneasiness.

This article intrigued her and she wondered if this threat was the norm prior to the commencement of the war, which began, for Canada on September 10, 1939.

She leaned back in her chair and glanced at Flynn's notepad. He'd written four names with accompanying information, but none with a wife named Anne. "How are you doing?" she said, not really questioning the lack of findings but felt the need to pause his search for the moment.

"About as well as you did earlier," he said, raising his hand and stifling a yawn. "I didn't realize how tiring research was." He leaned back and looked at her screen, the newspaper article she had found, and expanded it making it easier to read. "What have you found?"

"I was wondering, if there were many saboteur attempts in the years leading up to the war. After all, it was the perfect time. The United States had what they called fifth columnists, Nazi spies who conducted sabotage, hoping to weaken the Allied war effort."

Flynn contemplated that idea. "So, you think maybe that had something to do with our family's name change? Maybe my great grandfather was a spy." He laughed. "I hope not, for Gran's sake."

"Me too." Then a thought just occurred to her; she'd come across a similar situation years ago, and had forgotten until now. "What if Anne was married before and her husband died and she remarried in 1938 or 1939. That would explain her name changing, but it wouldn't explain why there is no marriage for her with a new husband, unless … they lived common law and didn't marry."

Flynn contemplated the idea. "Actually, I think that scenario is a much better one, although the war and spies might be more fun to look into.

So, how do you plan to find a previous husband when you don't know his name?"

"Probably the hard way; it'll take quite a while. I'll start by going through Ontario marriages with a two year plus or minus and just use the first name of the bride as Anne for 1936, and see what comes up and make note of all the possibilities. Then, I'll check those with the Canadian deaths and see if one of the husbands died between the marriage and 1940." Meg checked the grandfather clock on the far wall.

"But, perhaps tomorrow, it's getting late."

Flynn smiled. "Tomorrow, then. But in the mean time, I'll come by your house at nine. You might get a few things unpacked with the extra help."

Meg laughed at that. "Just getting the boxes *in* the house would be a great help. So, yes, I'll see you then."

Flynn watched as Meg's car backed up and then turned to drive through the gate opening, a small piece of paper with her address and phone number in his hand.

Feeling better, Alice had joined him at the door and he put his arm around her.

"I'm going to marry that girl," he said.

Alice raised eyebrows made him smile. "Oh, what does she say about that?"

"She doesn't know it yet."

Chapter 4

It was two o'clock in the morning, the light from a half-full moon shone through the window and across her bedspread, and Meg was still awake. The day's research was keeping her up, but if she was honest with herself, thoughts of Flynn also crept into her wakefulness. That in itself was disconcerting. She wanted to focus on her job, and having him help would be an asset, but working so close to him also unsettled her. He was attractive, charming and seemed to be interested in her, or maybe it was just his desire to help his grandmother find her family. Maybe he was just a player and liked to score another conquest, but she didn't think so. She'd find out more tomorrow.

Thinking over the different reasons why a family didn't exist before 1940, she dismissed all possibilities, for the time being, except one; that Anne had remarried and changed her name. That would be her focus for the next few days. It would take a while, as one-name searches always did, but she was hopeful.

It promised to be a beautiful day, sunny and a bit cooler, with a cloudless sky. She'd woken past her planned seven o'clock and had to rush to get herself ready before Flynn was due to arrive.

The doorbell rang and she ran to answer it, pulling a t-shirt over her head. Flynn was at the door with two take-out coffees in his hands. He smiled when he saw Meg. "Good morning." She opened the screen door for him and he stepped inside. "I'm glad I took the liberty," he said, noticing how tired she looked, and handed her one of the drinks.

"Thanks, I had a late night." He gave her a feigned scandalous look at that. She rolled her eyes and shook her head, then smiled. "I couldn't stop thinking of Anne and her possible other husband."

He laughed softly as he entered the living room, or what would be the living room once the crowded essentials were moved from the outer wall of the room and eventually placed in a better arrangement with their more decorative accessories. "You and me both, I couldn't sleep and spent a couple of extra hours checking out the spies and saboteur aspect."

"Did you find anything interesting?" She sighed, taking a sip of the rejuvenating brew.

"Surprisingly, I did; probably nothing important regarding our search, but I saved the page for you to see when we get back." He looked around her new home. "This is very nice. The house seems to have good bones and the yard is wide enough you could put a circular drive out front later if you like."

"That's actually a good idea, because the driveway now is very narrow and if I get clients, it wouldn't be an issue to get out."

She looked out the living room window and noticed he had parked along the side of the road across from her house.

"Are there large items in the bin?" he asked, joining her in her gaze. "Because I could call a friend to help me."

"No, just boxes. I hired a moving team for an hour to bring in some of the larger furnishings ..." she waved her hand about the room in illustration, "and the house came with appliances already."

"Great! Is the bin locked?" He began to head for the door. Meg pulled the key from her pocket and handed it to him before he opened the door.

Meg watched as he unlocked the bin and opened the doors wide enough to walk into. A moment later he was coming up the steps with one box balancing upon a slightly larger one. He'd worn a short-sleeved shirt and she noticed the muscles in his arms as she opened the door for him.

"Why don't you leave the door open, that way you can concentrate on unpacking," he suggested. After a nod in agreement, he moved the lever on the screen door allowing it to stay open enough for him to enter with a box.

By eleven o'clock the bin was empty and among the items stacked on the living room floor were the flattened remains of the bin's unpacked boxes.

The boxes had wisely been labelled and he had made several trips to her room with the bedroom boxes, and several more, smaller, heavier ones to the kitchen.

The day had grown warmer and with the house facing the east, the cloudless sky had made it warmer. Meg thought Flynn had to be warm too, and his face showed the look of exertion created by lifting heavy boxes.

"Let's take a break," suggested Meg. "Are you getting hungry?"

Flynn breathed a sigh. "I wouldn't mind a cool drink."

"Follow me."

Meg led the way to the kitchen. Skirting the number of boxes that sat stacked in the centre of the room, she went to the fridge while Flynn sat at the bar. She was rewarded with a smile when she turned back from the fridge with two bottles of beer in her hand.

"Just what I needed," said Flynn.

"I made sandwiches too, if you'd like one, shaved ham and Havarti cheese?"

"Yes, please."

Meg took one of the few plates that she had unpacked earlier and placed the chilled sandwich on a plate which she set in front of Flynn. "Mustard?"

"No, thanks, this will do," he said, biting into the sandwich with enthusiasm.

Meg laughed at his exaggerated enjoyment, glad too that he had come over.

She looked around at the dozen or so boxes that took up most of the kitchen's floor space, some of them, being too heavy for her to lift; she would have had to unpack slowly from the driveway, item by item. "Thanks for coming by and helping today, it would have taken me the rest of the week to unload that storage bin. As it is now, I can start to put things away more carefully."

"You're most welcome." He finished his sandwich then picked up his bottle of beer. "I saw a bench in the back yard earlier. Why don't we go outside and sit for a while."

"I think we could both use a rest." She turned and unlocking her sliding door that looked out over the back yard, led the way.

They sat companionably, watching the birds and the few butterflies that were attracted to a large butterfly bush that hugged one corner of the yard.

"Whoever lived here before must have loved their garden," commented Flynn. "There are a lot of different kinds of plants here. You should have colour all season long with the variety of perennials that are planted in these beds."

Bumble bees especially enjoying the dahlias that stood as a backdrop along the lot line, hummed their way back and forth across the yard, taking little heed of its human visitors. A central bed consisted largely of a huge hydrangea with its pinky-purple flowers, surrounded by shorter white flowers that Meg didn't recognize.

An arbour that led to a walkway down the side of the house was covered in trumpet vines. Flynn pointed to the vine now in bloom. "You'll probably get some humming birds and maybe even orioles coming to visit that one."

"Orioles?"

"Yes, it's actually quite entertaining to watch a bird try to get nectar from a flower."

A birdbath, placed beneath a shady tree that grew on the neighbour's side of the fence but was so large it hung over into Meg's yard, had a visiting robin who seemed to delight in the small amount of water that had accumulated after the rain from two days ago.

"It is lovely, isn't it. I think it was the garden that sold me on the house, to be honest with you."

They sipped their drinks, enjoying just being together outside.

Back at his grandmother's house, they parked their cars and walked through to the office area, Meg wondering where Alice was, but didn't want to ask.

Once seated Flynn scooted his chair closer to her so she could see the notes he had taken. "Just one in Ontario, besides the Grand Bend incident. This one involved the Niagara Falls Power plant in 1939." He pulled up the newspaper article on the screen so Meg could read it.

October 3 1939
A heroic act today, thwarted Nazi saboteurs' plans to bomb the hydro electric plant at Niagara Falls by Lieutenant William Carter while on patrol along the Niagara River. After an attempted murder upon one of his men, Lieutenant Carter caught up with the men responsible, before they

had time to place the explosives, they intended to use to destroy the plant. Carter took down one man after himself being fired upon and wounded. Aided by Parks police officer David Baker, the second suspect was shot after he trained his weapon upon the two men. Corporal Fenwick, rescued from the Niagara River, was able to tell of the saboteurs' assault; intending to kill him, before being rushed to the hospital with knife wounds. It is hopeful that Corporal Fenwick will be recovered sufficiently to testify at the trial. The defendant Hans Victor Schneider, formally a resident of Edmonton was arraigned earlier this day and will stand trial October 18 for sabotage and attempted murder.

"Wow, imagine what would have happened if they had succeeded?" said Meg.

Flynn agreed. "Yes, but that's not the interesting part. The same month I found this." He scrolled down to the next newspaper article he had saved, then turned the screen in Meg's direction. "This happened six days later."

October 9

At 7am today the body of Niagara Commission Parks police officer David Baker was found floating in the waters of Dufferin Islands. He had been dead for several hours; according to the coroner, and the cause is suspected homicide. Officer Baker was due to testify at the trial of accused saboteur Hans Victor Schneider.

"Then on the day of the trial I found this." He took back the computer, found the next page he had saved and then passed it back to Meg.

October 18

The trial of alleged Nazi saboteur Hans Victor Schneider began today in a Toronto courthouse. The defendant refused to have counsel and Lieutenant Carter was the only witness due to the deaths of Corporal Fenwick and Police Officer Baker earlier this week. The prosecutor had summed up his case by noon and tomorrow the defendant will have the opportunity to plead his case.

"So, both Fenwick and Baker were dead? That seems very suspicious."

"This was 1939. Do you think it might fit your new scenario?"

"You mean if Anne was married to either of the murdered men? It might, but I doubt it." She considered that scenario. "It would make the research easier, but it's a long shot."

Flynn was on a roll now and was eager to continue in this direction. Meg smiled; he'd caught the research bug.

"I think we should see if we can find them on a directory for 1939 or 1938."

"Ok, why don't you check the Ontario directories and I'll work on finding a marriage with the 'Anne' name idea and see if we can find a correlation."

"Great!" Flynn moved his laptop back along the table to allow enough space so Meg could use her writing pad and make notes.

It was one o'clock by the time Meg had entered Anne's name and the results came up—a lot of them. She kept the area confined to Ontario for the time being, hoping to find something relevant and to save time; considering she had to check death records once she had exhausted the marriages. But Anne was a very common name and unfortunately there were ten pages, which added up to just over two hundred results. This would take a while.

The familiar, coloured lights flitted across the table as they had done yesterday as the sun came around to the garden side of the house. Flynn was intent with his search into the directories stopping now and then to write down his findings.

"I found out how Corporal Fenwick died," he said.

Meg paused and looked at his screen. Apparent suicide, according to the coroner. She read the rest of the news article. He'd been shot and the gun was found in his hand when police arrived. She sat back, and re-read the article again. "That's very strange. Two witnesses turning up dead, just before a trial."

"I thought so," agreed Flynn. "And why they didn't look into it further, in itself seems strange, considering the circumstances."

"What happened to the third witness? the one that made it to the trial."

"I don't know, I haven't been looking for him."

Meg thought about the different ways they could look for this man. "If he was in the military, he may not be on any 1940 to 1945 directories, so start at 1946 and go up to 1950, and see if you can find him. I'll carry on with my marriages."

She laughed. "I only have a hundred more to do."

They were interrupted by a tap at the open door. Alice had decided to look-in on them. Flynn rose and went to his grandmother. "Come and sit with us for a while, Gran."

"Martha sent me in to see if Meg was able to stay for supper." She sat in Flynn's chair while he went to get another one that was by the wall.

"That's very kind, but ...," said Meg.

"Of course, she will," said Flynn. "Unless you have other plans?"

"Well, no, but ..."

"Good," said Alice. She looked around at the computer screens and the notes they had made. "Do you have time to go to the bakery, Flynn? I told Martha I felt like having meat pies for supper. Seeing she has to leave early tonight to take her husband to an appointment, I thought that would be the easiest meal for her."

"Sure, I can go now." He glanced at the results Meg was making note of. "Would you like to come along, it's not far. Your eyes must be getting tired."

Meg nodded and pushed back her chair. "I would like that. It would give us time to think too, and compare notes."

Alice took Flynn's arm and stood up. "Good. I'll let Martha know." Flynn held the chair as she turned to leave. "Perhaps get eight pies and some custard sliders for dessert as well. I'll give some to Martha for her and Tom; save her making something when she gets home."

Flynn clicked his heels and gave her an obedient salute. "We won't be long."

They took the same route as they had yesterday, but instead of crossing over the town's main road and on towards the lake, they turned right onto Centre Street, where shops of all kinds lined the sidewalks.

The bakery wasn't that far up on the right and when they arrived, the baker inside was adjusting his pastry goods in the display window. There were two customers ahead of them and while they waited Meg took the opportunity to look at all the treats offered behind the glass case that ran along the entire side of the shop.

Flynn purchased the meat pies and vanilla sliders his grandmother requested, then stood looking at all the pastries they didn't buy. "Anything else strike your fancy?" he asked, bending down to get a better look at the iced cakes in the back row.

Meg laughed softly to herself. "I was just about to say the same thing to you, but since you're asking." She pointed to the chocolate-iced cupcakes."

He laughed and asked the clerk to wrap up two more items, separately, so they could snack before returning back to the house.

They sat together on a bench outside the bakery, eating their chocolate cupcakes. It was considerably warmer now and tourists crowded the sidewalks on both sides of the street. "Oh my," said Meg. "I haven't had anything this yummy in quite a while." She looked thoughtfully at the store window. "I think I will get some to take home with me." She deposited her wrapper in the sidewalk garbage container, then went inside, leaving Flynn smiling on the bench while she made her purchase.

They walked back, happy in their mutual enjoyment of having discovered a similar liking. They hadn't spoken of their search results and Meg was glad that this time gave them the freedom to talk to each other without the pressure of research; plenty of time for that later once they were back at the house.

Walking back, Flynn paused in front of a house a little up the street from his grandmother's. "As a young boy I always thought this house was haunted, and that a witch lived there." He smiled at the telling. "My buddies and I would hide behind the fence here, just before sundown and wait, hoping we would see a ghost."

"What did your parents think of your ghost hunting expeditions."

He laughed. "I lived with Gran during the summer and as long as I was home when the street lights came on, she didn't comment much on our explorations of the town."

"Sounds like the perfect summer."

"It was," he said ruefully. "I wish now I had gotten to know my grandfather; but I was still quite young when he died." He smiled. "Apparently, I look a lot like him."

"That's nice." Meg looked at him considering. "I suppose on a positive note, you can see how your grandfather looked as he grew older, just by looking in the mirror."

He stopped, and looked at her, thoughtfully. "Yes, I guess that's true. I hadn't thought of it that way before. That's a lot to live up to. He was a wonderful man according to my father." Flynn shifted the boxes of bakery goods to his other hand. "Come on, let's get these to Martha."

Chapter 5

Flynn had continued his newspaper searches after supper and was enjoying the time looking through the old records. He'd checked earlier, through the available directories and had found both Fenwick and Baker and neither had been married prior to 1939. Then checking for Carter in 1946 to 1950 he found nothing, thinking perhaps he had died during the war.

"This is interesting," said Flynn. "I found the results of the trial."

Meg paused in her writing to listen. She was beginning to find the saboteur articles interesting as well.

"They had the trial. There was only the one witness, a Lieutenant Carter, who entered the courtroom with a cane and arm in a sling. The jury found Hans Victor Schneider guilty of sabotage and attempted murder and he was sentenced to death."

"Well, I guess, that's that. I wonder if they found out who murdered the Park police officer, and I suspect too, corporal Fenwick?"

"I went to the end of the year and found nothing about that. Maybe the next year. Do you think its worth continuing or are there other areas I could look into?"

Satisfied with the outcome of his newspaper searches, and having no results with the directory names, Flynn sat back so he could glance at Meg's computer screen.

Meg smiled. "You could start looking for the deaths of the husbands I have for all the Anne's I found, then we will see if any of them died prior to 1940. If you find one, it might support our new husband idea." She considered that for a moment and added, "We could check directories too, but the deaths would cover larger areas for us and cut down on time checking individual cities by years."

"Will do. What site do I use?"

"Start off with Family Search." She placed her written list closer so he could see the names she had listed. "I'm on Anne number 132, so when I've finished, I'll join you in the search."

Feeling hopeful, now with the extra help, Meg continued with the list of marriages for an Anne in Ontario.

It was Anne marriage number 141 that something seemed familiar. Flynn was busy making notes on his findings but looked up as she said his name.

"Have you found something?"

"What was the first name of that lieutenant who testified in the trial?"

Flynn checked his notes to make sure before answering. "William. William Carter." He leaned sideways to better see her screen. "Why, did you find him on a marriage record?"

"I think so. Anne Ramsey married William Carter, November 10, 1937, Niagara Falls, Ontario."

"So, that means he's my great grandfather?"

44

Meg smiled at that conclusion, a mistake that many novice researchers make. "Maybe; but not unless we can prove it. I need to check the actual record and see if Anne's mother's name is mentioned for a start."

She opened up the record of the marriage for William Carter and Anne Ramsey and scanned the page that gave the information about the bride and grooms family.

Sunlight had slowly moved to the back of the house and coloured lights from the bevels flickered across their work space. "Lillian," she said quietly, almost to herself.

Flynn was more definite about the find and said the name out loud, "Lillian Kelsey, mother. It has to be them. And if they were married in 1937, then William Carter is my grandmother's actual father, not Steven Hughes!"

"I'll admit it is starting to look like that, but we still can't assume that just yet." Meg jotted down the information in her notepad then actually printed out the document. "He was on a directory in 1939, but not on a 1940 one. Anne Hughes is on a 1940 directory but not on a 1939 directory."

"Do you still think he died and Anne remarried," he emphasised the word remarried with air quotes, "Steven Hughes?"

"Well, the most obvious reason for a death at that time would be the war, especially as we know he had the rank of lieutenant. I've checked for deaths in general for 1939-1940 but we haven't checked the military death records yet. If he's on them, then we know he died and it should also give us his family information. If he's not on them, then it means he didn't die as a war casualty. We won't be able to find him in the war unless we knew his regiment. Canada has fairly strict privacy rules."

Up to now she had made superficial searches through the indexed names until she had something more substantial to look into. "I think first, we have to go past the index for marriages and look into the actual records for all the Anne's I have and check for the bride's mother's name, and see if there are any more named Lillian."

"Great, show me which site and I'll work on half your list. And if William and Anne are the only couple, then what?"

"We check the war dead records, for William Carter. If he's not there then we have an interesting mystery." Another scenario would also explain the lack of a husband for Anne Hughes in 1940, but Meg was reluctant to mention it. She watched as Flynn dutifully set up his notepad ready to record any information he found, from the records he looked into, and decided she should share her idea. "Flynn, what if William Carter abandoned his wife in 1940, or was hurt somehow and had brain damage and didn't remember he was married. That would explain why she didn't legally remarry, not knowing what happened to him ... whether he was dead or not"

Flynn paused to consider that. "Well, I suppose I'd rather think of him as indisposed instead of a rotter who would abandon his wife and child." He smiled enthusiastically. "Hopefully, we'll find out."

By eight o'clock they had gone through all the marriages for Ontario and the death records for all the husbands married to an Anne, as well as the military death records. There were no other Lillians listed, as the mother of a bride named Anne, and no William Carter other than a seventy-six-year-old man from Kingston.

A shadow passed across the window and Flynn saw Martha carrying a tray to the back yard. "Gran must be in the back yard now, enjoying the last of the sun." He leaned back and pushed his chair away from the table. "Shall we take a break?"

Meg nodded in agreement. It had been a long day, but they had accomplished a great deal since yesterday.

The early evening was still warm, and the sinking sun still lit up the garden. Alice sat on a garden bench, a tray of tea and cookies beside her. Her face lit up when she saw Meg and Flynn enter the garden from the kitchen door.

"Come, join me." She motioned for them to take a seat on some patio chairs across from hers. "How are you two making out with the search?"

The grass was soft under her feet as Meg walked over and took the seat next to Alice. Flynn answered for them both, "Quite well actually, although we have encountered a bit of a conundrum."

Alice raised an eyebrow in question. "Well, it seems we found your mother and grandmother on

47

a marriage certificate." He hesitated, not sure what to say now.

"I hear a—but—there," said Alice.

"It's a bit complicated," continued Meg. "We found a William Carter, married to an Anne Ramsey, in Niagara. But, after 1939 William seems to have disappeared and Anne shows up as Anne Hughes in 1940 and there is no sign of an actual marriage to Steven Hughes."

"I don't understand..." Alice gave her a puzzled look. "Wait, you mean my father might not be Steven Hughes?"

"We don't know right now what to think," answered Flynn. "It seems to be a mystery."

"I wish I had more documents to help you," said Alice, her voice betraying her distress at the news.

Flynn came over and sat next to her, putting his arm around his grandmother. "Not to worry, Gran. We'll figure it out." He gave Meg a look and slight tilt of his head indicating they take a walk and discuss this revelation.

They were quiet until further up the street from the house. "What do you think?" asked Flynn.

"I'm not sure now. Up to now we've kept the search confined to Ontario. I will feel better if we expand the search for William to all of Canada now, including the marriage records. There's a small chance we might find another Anne with a mother named Lillian. With the records being closed that could hamper us, we'll have to be inventive."

"What about directories," he suggested.

"At least we will get an address for them while they were married," said Meg.

"Is it possible that someone who lives in their house now might have some information?"

Meg smiled at this suggestion. "You're getting good at this. We already have the addresses from their marriage record, for the bride and groom." She nodded. "It's a long shot, most would be dead by now or at least older than your grandmother, but worth a try, especially with the publicity he received because of the trial, someone in the area might remember a story or two."

"I think we will find out more though when we get the DNA results back," she added. "We may find actual relatives."

They had received the DNA kit quite quickly by courier. Meg and Flynn had sat Alice down at the dining room table and took her through the procedure required. Take this swab," instructed Meg, "and scrape it inside your mouth, around your left cheek for one minute." Flynn timed the task, and when completed took the swab and deposited into a small vial. "Now take this one and do the other cheek for a minute," said Meg.

Flynn repeated the steps and placed the two vials into a pre-addressed box. "There, done," said Flynn. "Now we just have to wait for the results."

It could take up to eight weeks—the instructions said, maybe less—to get the results back and then they would find out a lot more ... hopefully.

"I like the idea of a field trip," laughed Flynn. "The marriage certificate showed the addresses we need; one each for the bride and groom and their parents as well. We have three addresses to check now. Not sure what we will say though, to anyone we might find at those addresses."

"I suppose the truth, that we are researching the family that used to live here in the 1930s."

Flynn picked up the pace a bit, they passed the bakery and continued down the sidewalk until they came to a local park, one of three, that had a large wading pool in its centre. They sat under a tree on one of the many benches that dotted the park area.

"I'm starting to feel more enthusiastic now," he said, then added, "although this lost husband does seem unsolvable."

By two o'clock the next day they had left Alice's house and started on their quest, addresses in hand.

"There on the left, the big white house with the black trim," said Meg, who had the directions to the third house they would try. They had been to the addresses shown for the bride and groom's families, and now, the last house they would try was 47 Lawrence Street, the former home of the groom. There was a long wide driveway that curved towards the front of the house. A long wrap-around, covered veranda hugged the front and continued along one side of the building. They parked in what appeared to be the family's usual spot and Meg waved in a friendly greeting to a woman who sat on the veranda close to the front door. She sat in a wheelchair, and from a distance, seemed to be elderly.

Meg got out first and waited for Flynn to join her, and together they approached the short staircase that led to the veranda. The woman was in fact elderly and seemed to be in her eighties. She sat with a blanket across her lap and a shawl wrapped around her shoulders. "Hello," she said. Her voice was strong and confident and she smiled back at them. "Is there something I can help you with?"

Suddenly a younger woman came through the front door, a dish towel in her hands, as she dried them. "If you're selling anything, we're not interested," she said, in a dismissive tone.

"No," replied Meg, a little taken aback. "We were just wondering if you might know anything about the young man who used to live here in the late 1930s."

"No, I don't," answered the young woman.

"His name was William Carter," added Flynn.

The young woman, suspicious, looked at the older woman for direction. "It's all right Sally," said the elderly woman. "I'll speak to them now."

With a huff, the young woman, turned and went back to whatever she had been doing before being interrupted.

"Don't mind her." The elderly woman laughed silently, shaking her head. "She's supposed to be my personal support worker, but doesn't do much but complain. I'm replacing her tomorrow; I need a more cheerful person around me." She chuckled as she looked towards the screen door which her support worker had let slam. "Life is too short."

She straightened up and looked at her visitors. "My name is Dottie Cartwright. Please sit down and explain to me more about why you came here."

Meg and Flynn each took a wicker chair and moved them closer in a more favourable arrangement for conversation. Meg took the lead. After introducing themselves, she explained, "Flynn's grandmother wanted to know more about her father, William Carter. He seemed to have disappeared about 1940, and we're hoping someone near to where he lived back then might know something about him."

Dottie smiled. "You are in luck. I do know something about him. This house was his. My father was his best friend and William Carter gave this house to him when he went away. It always saddened my father, that he never saw his friend again. I don't know the details, but he left the area in a hurry and changed his name. He told my father he was sorry that they could never speak to each other again, and apparently my father never knew why, or at least he never talked about it. I think it had something to do with the war, but I don't know for sure. Maybe he was a spy for the military," she offered.

She looked around at the home she had known since her childhood. "My father was grateful to William until the day he died. They grew up together. Even though he had been offered a lot of money for this property, my father would never sell this house." Her eyes welled up. "He hoped one day William would come back and see him."

Meg felt her emotion and took her hand in hers. "I'm sure he would have if he could." She looked at Flynn, who looked saddened at her loss. "We are so thankful for this information. It will mean a lot to William's daughter."

The old woman smiled, happy that she could tell what she knew from years ago.

A shout from inside the house reached the veranda indicating that Dottie's lunch was ready. Dottie rolled her eyes. "I suppose I must suffer her cooking for one more day."

"Thank you," said Meg. "What was your father's name?"

"Henry Cartwright," she replied. "It was nice to speak to you. I'm afraid I must go now." The PSW opened the screen door and prepared to wheel Dottie into the house for her lunch. She gave a hostile glance at Meg and Flynn, before moving the chair from its place and wheeling it inside.

Meg and Flynn were left looking at each in disbelief. It was exciting and seemed unbelievable but at the same time made sense. So, William

Carter left the area, changed his name and moved on with his life.

"Do you think that means William Carter is actually Steven Hughes?" asked Flynn.

"It would explain a lot," said Meg, "but why would he do that?"

They talked as they went back to the car. "Maybe it had something to do with the saboteur."

Once in the car, Flynn paused before starting the ignition. "Where do we go from here, in research I mean. Did they have witness protection programs back then?"

Meg nodded, understanding the dilemma. "No, but I suppose the army could do something similar if they wanted to. I never like to assume anything, but we seem to have enough circumstantial evidence to carry on. If there are relatives on William's side who have registered with a family genealogy site, we might find proof in the DNA when it comes back. So, I think it's safe to carry on with William and Anne as your grandmother's parents—for now."

"The good news is that we are far enough back in time now, that we can search census records and marriages easier."

The motor hummed and Flynn leaned back. He reached over and gave Meg's hand a squeeze. "Thank you. I feel more hopeful now."

Chapter 6

October 1939 Niagara Falls Hospital

"Are you feeling better, Carter."

"Yes, Sir," responded Lieutenant William Carter. "They said I was lucky. It could have been worse."

Besides the injury to his leg from his struggle with the saboteur, the bullet had entered his side on an angle and hit his arm then exited without hitting any vital organs. He was shot at by an unknown assailant and it was obvious it was a comrade of the man facing trial in just another week.

"Will you be able to testify?"

Carter nodded. "If I have to be brought in on a stretcher, I will be there." Then his brows drew together in concern. "But I am worried about my family, Captain. I have had threatening notes; hateful messages, saying what they will do to my wife and child if I testify against their friend." He felt a lump in his throat at the memory. "There are too many of them."

His Captain smiled. "We will take care of that, Carter. You will be given a new name and your family will be relocated to Toronto. We have men watching your family home now and they will help with the move later this week. You will be given new documents; birth records, marriage records, identity records, but you must keep this secret, if it is to be successful. These men are not above using your friends or family members against you, to persuade you not to testify, and if you do there's the chance of revenge. No one must know. No one," he emphasized.

Carter didn't know what to say. He felt as if a weight had been lifted from him. He had been laying in the hospital bed wondering what to do once he had testified and the trial over. This would mean losing all the connections he had; friends, family … and starting over, but it would keep the people he cared about safe.

"Thank you, Captain. You don't know how grateful I am." The enemy were many and had infiltrated society. "But what if they are followed to the new home?"

"We will take care of that Lieutenant, the R.C.M.P. will provide several switches for the transport to Toronto. We have a home selected already. I would also suggest you try to not let reporters take your picture. We will try our best to prevent this as well. So far all they know is your name, so you need a disguise at the trial; maybe a mustache and glasses."

The captain smiled. "You are doing a service for your country. The least we can do is keep you and your family safe. Get some rest Lieutenant."

"Any word on Fenwick yet, sir?"

"The coroner has declared his death a murder now. At first, they thought it might be a suicide since the gun was found in his right hand,

and it was clear the gun had been responsible for the head wound on that side."

"What changed then?" asked Carter.

The captain smiled. "It was discovered that Fenwick was left-handed. The gun had been planted after his death in his right hand."

"You're the only witness now," said the captain. "It will take time to root out these spies and Nazi plants in the country. War is here, and to keep your family safe you will have to leave your old life behind. We will help you."

Carter nodded in compliance. The captain gave his shoulder a reassuring squeeze. "See you in court, Lieutenant."

2022 Niagara, Ontario, Canada

Alice met them at the door when they arrived back to the house, her face showing a hesitant hopefulness. She smiled though, when she saw Flynn and Meg. "You found something, didn't you?"

Flynn gave her a hug, his face alight with happiness for her. "Yes, Gran. I think we figured it out." He looked to Meg for confirmation. "We both feel William Carter and Anne were your parents, and that for some reason, they changed their name and moved to Toronto, where William wouldn't be found."

Alice's eyebrows raised a bit at that. There would be a lot of questions his grandmother would have. As they moved to the living room Flynn explained further, "We think it had something to do with a Nazi saboteur and a trial where William was a witness. We can't prove it for sure but we think the army protected him and his family from other threats during this time."

Alice sat silent while Flynn and Meg explained, her attention focused now on every word. "Well, that's a lot to take in, but it sounds as if he was a hero."

Meg took a seat opposite Alice. "We'll know for sure once we get the DNA results back. If there is a connection between you and another person on his side of the family, that will tell us if what we have concluded is true."

"For now, we can carry on and go back a few more generations and hopefully find some of his siblings, as well as your mother's side of your family. There should be a lot on the 1921 and 1911 census records, and there are a lot of birth and marriage records that should be available."

"For now, though, Meg has to go home and get some rest." Flynn gave Meg a questionable look. "Are you free for lunch tomorrow? We can get started after we eat."

Meg smiled, thankful that Flynn understood she had to get her thoughts together, not to mention she was still unpacking, and wanted to get her place in some kind of order.

"I'll be here at eleven," she said.

"One more to go," said Meg, quietly to herself. With Flynn's offer of the use of an office, Meg had left the unpacking and setting up of her office to the last. Her new home was a two-bedroom, one-level house, small, compared to the one she had shared with a friend in Grimsby, but it was cozy and all she really needed. The second bedroom made a perfect office; at the front of the house, it faced the morning sun.

While setting up her computer her mind wondered, contemplating the next steps they would take in searching for Alice's family. She was glad of the extra help and if she was being honest with herself, found Flynn's company pleasing. The longer they worked together, the more she noticed little things about him; his hazel eyes, the straight angle of his nose, his muscular arms that showed beneath his shirt, his ability to concentrate on their task and his love of family. She smiled to herself as she arranged the printer in its place on her desk. She wasn't deluded though, and had realized from the beginning that he had affected interest in his family genealogy just to spend some time with her, and she had accepted that pretense, interested in how it might play out. She'd noticed the look on Alice's face as he made that declaration and felt she had an ally in that department. Perhaps later she would talk to Alice alone and get some further information, but for now she would enjoy the attention he was paying her, as they focused now on Alice's family, confident that their findings would be proven out by the DNA results that she expected to arrive within a few weeks.

Meg sat at her desk, a notepad by her hand. She would start with the marriage record and work backwards now knowing the names of William's parents, looking for any birth, death, marriage and census records for the direct line, going back as far as she could.

Perhaps they would find some immigration records at some point and be able to go back further if the family was from another country originally. Then they would do the same for the bride's family. After hours of looking and printing out record sheets they would have an ancestral history to give to Alice, hopefully augmented with newspaper finds and grave inscription information, perhaps even some military discoveries. She was excited now and couldn't wait to work on this project with Flynn. Once everything came together, perhaps she could help him search for his mother's side—the Flynn family in Scotland.

The next morning brought a chill to the air and a fog over Niagara. She drove carefully along the lake road, until she got to the road that linked Alice William's street, with the main street of town. It was almost eleven when Meg pulled into the driveway. Flynn was waiting by the door ready to greet her.

Meg smiled suddenly realizing she had hoped he would be waiting for her. "Good morning," she said, noticing he had a different look this morning. She looked at him, her eyes scrunched, pretending a critical evaluation. A day's growth of beard suited Flynn, giving him a sort of rakish appearance. "I like it," she laughed, then said, "How is your grandmother, this morning?"

Flynn opened the door and followed Meg into the house. "A little puzzled by what we said yesterday, but also excited that we might be able to continue now to find her family. I suppose my family too," he added. "She'll join us for lunch later."

"Martha's making some lunch for us, but we have time to figure out a research strategy first, unless you have figured out already how to proceed."

"Lunch would be nice," replied Meg, "and yes, I did give our plan of attack some thought last night."

Flynn took her jacket, and hung it up in the entryway closet, then they proceeded right to the office area to get started before lunch. Meg took out her laptop computer and placed it in her usual spot, then opened up her notepad to the page listing her plan. "I think we should probably cover two different sites and search for the same thing, that way we will be double-checking the information and also possibly find something important on one site that might have been missed on the other." Flynn nodded in agreement. "So, we can start with the marriage record." Meg looked around the room. "Do you have a large white board or perhaps a large sheet of paper we can use to start drawing up a family tree chart?"

Flynn answered immediately. He had seen some large rolls of craft paper in the basement. "Gran has some white rolls of paper, she's been saving. The local church used them to cover their tables during luncheons and asked her to store them several years ago, but they've gone to tablecloths now and haven't used them since."

"Sounds perfect. Can I help you bring one upstairs."

He was on his feet ready to retrieve the paper, before Meg could move her chair. "I'll get the paper if you set up my computer for me," he said as he left the room.

A soft thump alerted Meg to something outside. She'd heard that sound before at her other home and rushed out of the room, leaving a startled Martha who was coming in from the vegetable garden in wonderment. It was lying on the grass, hopefully just stunned and not damaged. A small yellow and black bird—a goldfinch.

Carefully she picked up the bird to examine it. The wing and legs didn't seem broken and its head seemed upright and not bent which might have happened after hitting the window. The bird sat still in her palm; it seemed unafraid and slightly dazed.

Flynn came back with a rolled-up piece of paper—three-feet wide, and when unrolled would cover the balance of the table-top area—to find Meg gone.

He saw her shadow cross the back yard window and realized she was outside. He set the paper down and went to see what had happened. Watching from the doorway he smiled, as Meg placed the bird gently on the garden table.

"What have you found?"

"A little guy, who hit the window," said Meg, as she watched the bird.

"Our neighbour has a large bird feeder; the goldfinches love the Niger seed he puts out." As if hearing about the food next door, the bird raised its wings stretching, and flew off to the neighbour's yard. Flynn saw the delight that came over Meg's face at the site of the bird's recovery, and found that touching. She was beautiful, he thought. The steel blue of her shirt matching the blue of her eyes.

A call from the kitchen announced lunch was ready. Flynn and Meg opted for eating theirs out in the garden at his grandmother's urging, while Alice sat and enjoyed her sandwich with Martha.

The sun was in the southeast still and hadn't fully reached the back garden. It was a beautiful English style garden. There were many perennials; most had finished their blooms by now but added the greenery as a backdrop to the annuals that hugged the edges of the garden. Two fanciful fairy statues stood in prominent places while a bench and small table stood in a spot where the visitor could overlook the whole of the garden from a different angle.

They sat together, enjoying the sunshine, the fog having been burned off. The bees hummed as they explored the variety of flowers, and birds flew back and forth from the safety of their trees.

"This is beautiful," said Meg. She took a bite of her sandwich, then threw a bit of crust towards a sparrow that was searching for something to eat under a nearby shrub.

"I've always loved this yard," said Flynn. "I think it's one reason Gran has resisted leaving this house to downsize. As long as she has Martha and can afford to hire garden maintenance, she will stay."

"If she ever does decide to sell, I would like to buy it from her," he said. He looked around. "I can picture myself living here."

"I'm sure she'd feel happy, knowing that it was being looked after by someone in her family. Where do you live now?"

"In Welland. I'd like to live closer, maybe the Chippawa area or Virgil."

Flynn set his plate down, his sandwich barely touched. Meg was watching the birds that had come closer with the offer of food.

"Meg, would you care to have dinner with me sometime?"

She suddenly turned and faced him, the crust in her hand forgotten for the moment. She laughed softly. "I've *been* having dinner with you, here."

He laughed too. "I mean, just the two of us."

That surprised her, but she liked this man, and nodded. "I'd like that."

"Is tonight too soon?" She could see the slight blush on his face as he looked at her hoping he hadn't ruined things by changing their relationship.

"Tonight, would be fine." She smiled at him. "Come on, let's work for a while first." She stood up taking her plate and drink with her.

Back inside, Flynn showed Meg his find from the basement.

"Perfect," said Meg when she saw the size of the paper. "We can make necessary notes too, as we go along." Meg started the chart off by writing in Alice's information in the centre of the sheet. Up from that, she drew a vertical dotted line going to her father and mother—William Carter and Anne Ramsey—dotted until the fact of parentage was proven.

They each had a printed copy of the marriage certificate of William and Anne. "Here you look for Anne Ramsey born 1915 on the 1921 census, and see if you can find the family. Remember her mother's name was Lillian Kelsey, but we also have her father's name now too— Edward Ramsey."

She passed Flynn her password information for the site he would use, while she checked another site for the same person. By three o'clock they had found Anne Ramsey and her family living in Cambridge Ontario.

By four o'clock they had found the parents of William Carter and his siblings living in Niagara Falls in 1921. Their marriage also in Niagara Falls produced their ages and the name of their respective parents—Alice's great grandparents.

Meg had recorded their finding on the chart paper in the form of a family tree. In a few hours they were able to go back three generations, to Flynn's 3x great grandparents.

"This is amazing," said Flynn. "How far do you think we can go back?"

"For Canada, maybe 1851, but if they came here from Britain, maybe much further."

By seven, they were sitting at a family-style, dinner-table at *Oh Canada Eh*? watching a comedy musical show.

"This is so good," said Meg. She took another spoonful of their split pea soup.

"You know, I've seen the ads and often thought of coming here."

She smiled at Flynn who was enjoying his own bowl of soup. "It's funny, but I suppose true; you seldom go and visit the wonderful attractions in your own back yard, unless perhaps you have visitors from another country and take them to see the sites. I think I was ten the last time I went on the Maid of the Mist, and that was only because my class went, not because my parents took me."

"It's true, same with my family. Although the Maid of the Mist is now the Hornblower." He looked around watching all the other guests that sat at similar tables. "This is my first time here too."

Suddenly some of the staff took their places on stage and their tribute to the musical Rose Marie began.

Halfway through, the musical review paused for a break while the main course was served.

During the meal, the staff approached several male guests to see if some were interested in participating in the next act.

Their tall server came over to Flynn and at his nod of consent, gave him a child's hobby horse to hold; that he would need in the show.

At the signal, the men chosen, stood up and at the urging of the crowd, they took the stage and joined the two actors dressed as Mounties, hobby horse in hand.

The music began; playing The Mountie Song, and all the amateur actors followed along, joining in the song and pretending to ride their noble steeds, all except one man, who didn't appear to know what the hobby horse was for, and instead of riding the horse like the other Mounties, happily waved his over his head. The crowd erupted in laughter.

Once the number was finished the crowd applauded their effort and each actor returned to their table.

Meg was still laughing as Flynn sat back down beside her. "That was wonderful," said Meg.

He smiled. "It was fun. I love that song."

It was nine-thirty by the time they had left the show and stood by the car ready to leave, enjoying the warm night. The dew had left a mist on the car and the air felt a bit damp. "Thank you for tonight," said Meg. "It's been a while since I enjoyed an evening out as much."

"I'm glad, I had a good time too." Flynn took her hand in his and drew her to him. He smiled softly, looking into her eyes, then leaned in to kiss her. A soft, firm, thorough kiss that Meg reciprocated.

"Oh," she said, once the effect had faded. Then she smiled and reached out to touch his cheek. "I wasn't quite prepared for that, could we maybe try it again?"

"I'd like that."

Chapter 7

It was three in the morning and Meg hadn't yet fallen asleep. Thoughts of the evening with Flynn had kept her awake. She hadn't realized how much she would enjoy his company beyond their collaboration in Alice's family history, not to mention the instant chemistry from their kiss, and second extended kiss. He was fun and didn't take himself too seriously. Not for the first time she wondered why a good-looking man like Flynn was unattached, but then in all fairness he could claim the same of her. Maybe she would have a quiet chat with Alice when Flynn wasn't around, if an occasion presented itself.

Such an occasion came about the next morning as Alice awaited her arrival at the front door.

"Good morning," said Meg.

Alice noticed her look past the door, puzzled that Flynn wasn't there. "Flynn was called away to help with some problem at work," she explained, as she stood back to allow Meg to enter.

"Oh, that's fine. I'm sure I'll be able to get a lot done today."

"Do you mind some company for a little while; Martha won't be in until noon today."

Meg hung up her jacket as Alice closed the door. "Not at all. I'd welcome your input." Then she smiled to herself. "And, we can chat a while."

Alice took up Flynn's place at the table, while Meg set up both computers; Flynn's just in case Alice wanted to participate. "I'm glad you have time to sit and talk about the search so far, I'm afraid we upset you yesterday with our declaration about William Carter possibly being your father. What we didn't explain very well, is that we think William Carter and Steven Hughes are one in the same."

Alice looked at her, taking in what Meg had just said. "So, that means Steven Hughes was still my father?"

"Yes, we think so, but there still has to be some proof for us to be sure of it. I'm hoping the DNA test will bring up something positive, which would give us that proof."

Alice looked at the chart that Meg and Flynn had started to work on, amazed at the names they had entered so far. "I never knew any of these people. No one ever spoke of them either." She gave Meg a concerned look. "Isn't that rather unusual?"

"I think so, but who knows what rules applied back then to military men and women. People in Britain who worked in the secret service couldn't speak of the work they did because they were bound by the Official Secrets Acts. Maybe something similar applied here too. I don't know."

Alice nodded in understanding, then switched the subject. "Flynn was sorry he couldn't be here today."

The conversation, now focused on Flynn, it was Meg's opportunity to find out more about him. "What does Flynn do?"

"Oh, he works for ... let me think—the Ministry of Mines—he's a geologist. The time he spends here is his vacation." She smiled. "He comes here every year at the same time for his time off, to be with me for three weeks and help around the house with things I can't manage."

Meg smiled at that. "That's nice of him. He's a very nice guy."

Alice gave her a knowing look. "I assume you knew he used his interest in family history as a ruse to get to know you better." Then she laughed when she saw Meg smile. "He wasn't very subtle, was he."

"No, but that's okay. I was hoping to get to know him, too." Alice smiled at that.

There was a question she was dying to ask and after a moment she decided to just come out with it. "Why is he still single?"

Alice looked at her, and chuckled softly. "Funny, he was thinking the same thing about you. You're a beautiful, successful woman."

Meg raised her eyebrows at that. "Really. Hmm ... well, I suppose I just never found the person I wanted to spend forever with." Then she laughed to herself.

"Exactly," agreed Alice. "Some people settle because they either can't be by themselves and are afraid to wait, or because they haven't had enough experience to know true love."

"You and Flynn seem to know what you want, maybe it will be each other, maybe it won't." She smiled and patted Meg's hand in reassurance. "I hope it will be."

With nothing more to say, Meg switched the topic back to Alice's family. "Would you like to help look for more information about your great grandparents?"

"Yes, I'd like that, but I don't know too much about computers."

"Not to worry, I'll show you."

It was several hours later that Flynn found Meg and his grandmother sitting in the back-yard garden, enjoying a glass of cool, white wine before supper.

He stood by the door watching the two interact and found it heartwarming. "Well, here are my two favourite ladies," he said, crossing the lawn to take up a place on a lawn chair he pulled up opposite them. "What a day, Gerald had a problem with an important mining claim. Thank goodness we got it figured out in time or I'd be in Toronto for the next two days."

He looked at the two women, wondering why they were outside, seeming to be enjoying the late afternoon together. "What have you two been up to today?"

Alice was the first to answer his question with an enthusiastic answer. "With Meg's help I was able to find my mother's grandmother's marriage record and hence her parents. We actually have some Irish on her side of the family." She glanced at Meg. "It was wonderful seeing how to find out information." Then considering, she added, "It gives you more of a connection to the past, a sense of belonging to something larger, an idea of your place."

"That's wonderful," said Flynn.

Alice glanced at the kitchen window, noticing Martha beginning to prepare supper. "I don't feel like a lot for supper tonight. I'll just have a bite with Martha and call it a night. It's been a long day for me. Why don't you two go out and enjoy supper together." Meg and Flynn both looked at Alice at the same time, then smiled at each other.

"Done," said Flynn. "Give me twenty minutes to clean up first."

At age eighty-four, Meg realized that anything out of routine can be stressful and tiring but that was not the case this time. Alice and Meg smiled at each other and at the scenario they had planned prior to Flynn's return home. Knowing what she did of Flynn's plans and interest in Meg, Alice had no problem encouraging the relationship. They had had a lot of time to chat during the afternoon and with Alice's assistance, Meg had agreed to join in her plan.

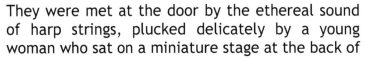

They were met at the door by the ethereal sound of harp strings, plucked delicately by a young woman who sat on a miniature stage at the back of the room.

"This is beautiful."

"It is nice isn't it. Whenever Gran and I sometimes go out for supper, this is our go to place."

"It reminds me of a Yorkshire pub I was once in. I don't remember seeing this place here before. Is it new?"

"It's fairly new. The owner has British roots and wanted an authentic pub; so, he went to England and bought one, had it dismantled and sent back to Canada, then had it reassembled. It took almost a year to reconstruct it, as it was in England.

The smell of fish and chips filled her senses as they passed the table of an elderly couple.

"It smells like the menu is authentic too."

A young man seated them in a small booth flanked on either side by panels of stained glass in wooden frames which acted as dividers between booths and gave the illusion of further privacy. Light from the low hanging lamps in the room provided enough light to illuminate the scenes of the coloured glass.

They sat opposite each other as each was given a leather-covered menu folder.

"It must have cost a fortune to recreate this." Meg looked around the pub admiring the character of the restaurant. "Well, I'd say, it was well worth it. I can't wait to taste the food."

Flynn smiled, pleased that he had thought to bring her to some place special. "How was your afternoon with Gran?" he asked, not looking up from his menu.

Meg noticed the small upturn of his lips, as he tried not to betray humour in his question.

"Very interesting and ... informative," she replied, also feigning interest in her menu.

Flynn set down his menu, containing all the restaurant's authentic culinary dishes. He smiled at her and waited for her to catch his eye. "I have something to tell you."

She looked up and gave him a stern look. "Is that where you tell me that you really didn't have an interest in family genealogy, but actually said so, just so you could spend time with me?"

He gave her a sheepish look. "Yes. You forgot to add the part about me fabricating an office space so you would work at Gran's place, or did she not tell you that part?"

Her expression didn't change as she studied his face. A handsome face she decided, the colours in his hazel eyes reflecting the matching brown and green checks of his shirt. His dark, brown hair, worn perhaps a bit too long, hung over his forehead, and he gave it a brush away from his eyes as he waited for her to speak.

"I do apologize for the deception, and for the most part it is true, but thanks to you that's changed ..." He paused as their waitress stood by their table, notepad in hand. After ordering and she left, he continued, "I really want to help Gran find her family ... and..." He looked at her and smiled. She set her menu down as well and looked at him, the scolding look from before now softened. He reached across and took her hand in his. "I wanted to spend time with you."

"Well, I have a confession too …" Meg started.

"Oh, you do?" She heard the laughter in his voice.

"Yes, I guessed your ruse from the beginning, and … I enjoy your company too."

His face relaxed. She placed her free hand on top of his and felt the energy of his touch on her and he returned the feeling with a slight squeeze. "I'm glad."

"I have some news," he said. "I will be able to extend my vacation for the remainder of the summer as long as I am available on call for any difficulties that come up. So, I will still be able to help you."

The waitress returned with their orders of fish and chips and placed each in front of them.

"Good," said Meg. "I can't wait to finish this search for your grandmother."

"Did you and Gran actually do any researching yesterday?"

Meg laughed softly. "Surprisingly, yes … well, a little," she amended. "You remember we had found William and Anne's families on the 1921 census form and William's parent's marriage, so we knew their names."

"Alice decided that she would like to know more about her aunts and uncles, so we spent time looking into William and Anne's siblings." She drew attention to the chart on the table where she had added the names of Alice's two sets of grandparents and their children."

Flynn scooted his chair closer to Meg's so he could see her computer screen easier. She'd entered the findings also on a computer family genealogy program that gave more details than appeared on the general working chart before him.

"Anne had two younger brothers—twins, who both died during the 1918 flu epidemic. She had two sisters; Elizabeth and Sarah and an older brother Edward, but we couldn't find much about him after 1921. I'll have to go into the Canadian war records again later to see if I can find him. He may have died in the war or even moved out of province." She switched pages now to the Carter

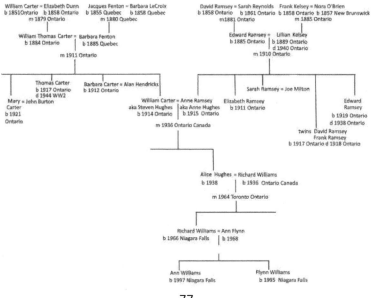

family. "William, on the other hand, had a brother and two sisters in 1921—a Mary and a Barbara. Barbara was a few years older than William and we found her marriage in 1934 to an Alan Hendricks." She pointed out the ages of each of William's siblings. "There is quite an age gap between the last child and Thomas so there may have been another child who died young."

"That's a great start," said Flynn, fascinated now that they could put names to these ancestor members. "I bet Gran enjoyed that."

"She did ..." said Meg, remembering the look of awe on Alice's face when she saw the actual census records. "... and even got a bit teary at the news about the twin boys. There had been an obituary for them in the paper ... quite touching."

He gave her a warm smile. "I'm ready to find out more. Where do we start today?"

"I think we will go back using the census records first to get names and locations, before branching out into marriages and deaths. We can check for newspaper listings too, after we get a rough picture for each family we find, using places and dates to help us."

Flynn nodded in acceptance of the plan and pushed his chair back to his place. "Shall I work on Anne or William?"

Meg passed her notes about William over to Flynn. "Start with William's parents. We have their names and ages so you can go backward from there. Remember," she reminded him, "when you find something, besides printing out your finds, take a full screen shot of the records, so we can go back later to document the source and buy certificates if needed."

Flynn was aware as to how the records worked now and Meg was happy to have another person there to hunt with her, as well as having Flynn's company, for his own sake.

Flynn gave her a mock salute and smiled, eager to start.

It was an hour later that they heard a tentative knock at the door to their office. Even though it was open, Martha stood by the door. "There's a phone call for you, Flynn."

"Uh—oh. Now what's happened?" he said. He muttered something under his breath as he pushed his chair back. "I'll be right back."

He was back, within minutes, but didn't look too happy. "I have to leave," he said. He stood in the doorway.

Meg could tell he was upset about leaving so abruptly. "It may take a week." He shook his head slowly. "I have to leave now. I'm sorry."

Meg got up and joined him. He pulled her close and gave her a warm embrace. "Where do you have to go?" she asked, once released.

"Iroquois Falls. They have a plane for me at the airport."

"Well, that's one good thing, you don't have to drive far."

"True." He smiled, then leaned close and gave her a lengthy kiss goodbye. "I have your number; I'll keep you updated." With that he was gone.

Meg could hear his car engine as Flynn left for the local airport and suddenly felt a little lonely. It was different in her house with her usual items before her while hunting for ancestors, but here without him to talk to was different somehow, as if she could physically feel his absence.

"Do you mind if I watch for a while?" came a voice by the door. Alice smiled and joined her taking up Flynn's usual place.

"It's not the same, is it?" she said. "I feel it too, when his vacation is over and he goes back to work. Mind you, he does visit throughout the year but it's not the same as having him live here."

"I suppose you must get lonely sometimes."

"Well, I have Martha. We've formed a close friendship over the years but she does have a family to take care of, now that she has grandchildren. And sometimes my son and his wife come by, but it's a fair distance from here to Winnipeg."

She smiled somewhat ruefully. "At my age, one doesn't have too many hobbies to keep busy with, but I do enjoy reading." She glanced at the site Meg had up on her screen.

Meg understood completely and returned her smile. "I'm checking out William's father's family. Would you care to watch."

"I'd like that very much."

It was shortly after nine o'clock, when Meg heard the ping of her phone indicating she had a message. It was Flynn. The message was short but reassuring:

Hi,

The plane ride was fine, had to wait a bit at the airport. Long drive in to the project. Just got settled into my room which I share with a guy named Frank ... hope he doesn't snore.

Say 'Hi' to Gran for me and let her know I arrived okay. The cell phone signal is spotty so may not be able to message for a while.

I miss you.

It was so refreshing to find a man who didn't play games. I miss you too, thought Meg, then typed that in her response, hoping he would get her reply.

Her office area was set up now in her spare bedroom and she would feel more at ease working here now, but thoughts of Alice—who also missed Flynn—changed her mind and she decided to return back to the makeshift office in the library. She'd had a restless sleep and thoughts of Flynn had kept her mind busy, thinking, playing out all potential situations. *"I miss you."* He had responded with a happy face emoji.

Chapter 8

She arrived shortly after lunch and found Martha and Alice in the garden enjoying the warm day.

At their wave, she joined them under the shade. "Have you heard from Flynn?" asked Alice.

"Yes, he said to let you know he arrived safely and that cell phone reception was sketchy." She smiled thinking of the message from last night. "I'll let you know if he sends another message."

"I'm glad," said Alice. "It's rather quiet around here without him."

Meg took a chair and moved it closer to the two women. "Would you care for a cool drink, Meg?" offered Martha.

"Thank you, that would be nice." The day had been getting increasingly warmer, and with it the humidity. The only relief in the garden was the shade provided by the old trees. Meg noticed the chirping of the birds at the feeder next door, and thought about the small goldfinch she had found, hoping it had survived.

"I thought I'd come by and work here today, perhaps provide a bit of company."

Alice smiled at her. "That was kind of you. How is your unpacking going?"

Martha returned with a glass of lemonade and handed it to Meg before taking up her seat again.

"I've got all the boxes unpacked now, it's just a matter of finding places for things to go. Flynn saved me a few days work by bringing the boxes in for me." She took a sip of the cool beverage. "I still have a few items and accessories yet to buy."

"I have some older furnishings stored in the basement, if you'd care to have a look. Most belonged to my mother, and I have no need of them now. If you see something you can use, you're more than welcome to have them."

Meg was touched by the offer and whether vintage furniture—for surely if they belonged to Alice's mother, they would be over sixty years old—would fit her home she would have to see. "I'd like very much to see them."

"Let's finish our drinks then we can go and take a look," said Alice, pleased that someone might find some use for items she had been saving for so long.

The basement had a high ceiling, unusual for this type of home and had just a few lights in critical areas. She could tell that it was used mainly as a storage area. A dehumidifier could be heard running in the room adjoining the furnace area.

The white of the kraft paper rolls stood out from the rest of the brown wooden furnishings. The floor was a smooth concrete and the items, Meg supposed to have once belonged to Anne Carter, stood on wooden skids to avoid possible water damage, if the sewer should back up.

"These are beautiful," said Meg, admiring a writing desk that sat at the head of a small walkway someone had formed with the furnishings so they could be viewed and handled more easily.

Alice smiled at that and encouraged Meg to take her time and assured her she was welcome to take any of the items she might use. "No one else in the family has a use for them; I've asked a few times over the years. People seem to like the more modern clean look of glass and metal."

"I love history as you might have guessed, and wooden furniture like this is just the thing for bringing history alive." Her hand passed gently over the smooth wooden top of the desk. It would be perfect in her hallway. "And that clock! It has to be late 1890s. It's German, isn't it?" The wall clock, was stored lying down on top of a side board, and had a beautiful eagle decorating the top and finials at the side and bottom.

"I'm not sure. No one ever said," offered Alice.

Meg touched the glass door which protected the cream-coloured face, branded with a symbol of two crossed arrows. "My grandfather had a similar clock, but when he died it went to my cousin.

"Well, then," said Alice, delighted in Meg's reverence for the clock. "By all means, it shall be yours."

"What about the side board or desk?" suggested Alice.

"I don't have a dining room set as yet, but it is beautiful and would give me a place to put my linens." Meg tested the drawers and found them deep enough to hold a variety of items that were currently sitting in a box against the dining room wall. The dark walnut would be easy to match, and she had a mirror that would look good on the wall above it.

"Are you sure?" she asked. "Wouldn't Flynn or his sister like to have them?"

Alice smiled and shook her head, indicating she'd asked them before. "They have no use for them, and I'd really like you to have them."

Meg smiled back. "I'd love them, and I promise to take good care of them."

"Good. Spend some more time rummaging around. There are also dishes and cutlery and some wall decorations. There might even be some linens you can use. They might not be your style, but Martha says I already have enough dishes, so look around and see what else you can find."

With that, Alice left Meg to rummage around while she went back upstairs to join Martha in the garden.

That afternoon, Meg had hired the two moving men she had previously used to help with the larger items in her home, and now stood with Alice and Martha as they moved the items Meg had chosen to take to her home: the desk, the sideboard, a bed headboard, the German clock, two small side tables and a few boxes of assorted smaller items. The basement seemed suddenly empty with just a few of Anne's things remaining.

"Thank you, again. I can't wait to see how they will look in my house. When Flynn gets back, you will have to come over and see where I've put them."

"I'd like that. Have you heard from Flynn lately?"

It had been three days since he'd left. "No, but he said cell phone reception was next to none where he was."

Four days later, Meg had completed her search for Alice's family. She had lucked out and found a Quebec site that had more information than she thought possible considering the years involved.

She had the computer genealogy filled out with all her results and now just had to provide her computer-illiterate client a complete family tree written on the large piece of kraft paper she had cut from the larger roll in the basement. Once done, she would present to Alice and Flynn the family members she had discovered. Flynn would enjoy the computer-generated family tree and all the extra information gleaned from newspapers and historical accounts that accompanied the different names, while Alice would enjoy following her ten generations back—as far as 1658 on her father's side—simply listing birth, marriage and death information. Meg had a binder with the relevant census records and a few pictures and would leave it up to the two of them to decide if they wished to order birth, marriage or death certificates.

Now completed, she would return home and begin working on her new commissions while waiting for Flynn to get back so she could present her finding to both of them at the same time. She was lucky, her online advertisement for genealogy research had generated two more clients, both eager to delve into their family tree.

She had to admit she had missed Flynn more these last couple of days. Focused once more on her task, she had actually, if she was being honest, accomplished more without him helping. Whether it was the distraction of him sitting next to her that kept her from her usual doggedness she wasn't sure … probably.

Flynn had finally been able to text her, updating her as to how things were going on his end. He'd hoped to be back before she had finished, but understood too she had other clients to consider and needed to complete the work before moving on.

It was two days later during her lunch that she had a message saying Flynn would be home by supper time the next day. Meg felt her heart beat quicken as she read the note. She felt the excitement … one more day.

The metal gray sky didn't look as if the rain would end soon. Meg was glad that lightning hadn't accompanied the storm which might have interfered with Flynn's flight, causing delays. He'd texted her once he was at the airport. Ten more minutes and he'd be home. Was it too forward for her to be waiting for him, maybe, but she didn't care. Six days without him told her all she needed to know. Did he feel the same? She'd know soon enough. She stood, with the umbrella Alice had given her, under the front entrance overhang, waiting. Drops, as they hit the metal eave troughs combined into a stream of water that puddled at the base of the vertical pipe that extended beyond the steps.

His car pulled into the driveway past the metal gates and parked in his usual spot. She waited as the engine stopped, the rain coming down harder now. He smiled when he saw her, and her heart warmed at the sight. Her heart suddenly quickened, as she opened up the umbrella, and ran to the car, careless of the puddles she stepped in. He undid his seat belt and smiled when he saw her standing there, umbrella in hand, drops sliding off the edges, ready to shelter the both of them from the rain.

Once out of his car, Flynn drew her in close and gave her a firm hug and equally firm and passionate kiss. She let the umbrella fall, not caring as it hit the ground and wrapped her arms around him for a warm embrace. They stood in the rain, their arms around each other. "I've missed you so much," he whispered to her.

"Me too."

She glanced at the front of the house and saw that Alice had come to greet Flynn as well, and was now smiling. "We're attracting attention."

Meg unfurled the final result of her research, the white kraft paper resisting the impulse to curl by the weights she had placed at each corner. Flynn and Alice sat opposite her along the side of the large table.

She smiled at Alice. "I've been able to go back ten generations on your father's side to 1658." Alice turned to look at Flynn, she smiled at him in disbelief.

"This is amazing!" she said. She leaned forward to follow along the chart as Meg slowly went through the numerous generations she had found.

"Your mother's family only went back to 1710, but both sides had some interesting ancestors." She smiled with her eagerness to explain a couple of very interesting facts. "I think you could apply for a membership to ..." she checked her notes before continuing, "... the 'La Société des Filles du Roi et Soldats du Carignan', which roughly means—the society of the Daughters of the King and the Carignan Soldiers, who were sent to new France to fight the Iroquois."

The look of amazement on her face warmed Meg's heart. Flynn gave his grandmother's hand a joyous squeeze. "This is so interesting!" he said.

"Who are the daughters of the king," asked Alice.

"Ah, the King's Daughters were about seven hundred young women who were sent to New France between 1663 and 1673, to marry colonists or soldiers who protected the colony. They were usually single women and many were orphans but some were widows. The King paid for their passage and also provided a dowery for each woman. It was part of his program to settle the colony in the new world." She pointed out the couple on her chart— Jacquette Michel and Andre Lagace married in 1668. "With this documentation you can apply for membership in this society."

Alice and Flynn traced her father's line back to this couple. "It says they were both born in France," said Alice.

"Yes," agreed Flynn. He gave Meg a questioning look. "Do you think I might be able to find their ancestors in France?"

"I'm sure you will find something, and there are various French research sites I can give you. Also, like most countries there are many Family History Societies you can join."

"Now, on your mother's side ..." Meg pointed out the marriage of a couple in 1785. "... a couple who were married in a Mohawk church which to me implies that possibly the bride was a Mohawk woman."

"Wow," said Alice. "This is much more than I had expected. Imagine all this information being available, so far back."

"We were just lucky that Quebec records are so extensive. Now, on your mother's, mother's side, I wasn't able to go back further than 1810, and they seemed to have come from the United States, so it's possible they were Empire Loyalists, but I can't prove it for sure."

"Well, I think you've done wonders." Her face showed disappointment for a moment before disappearing. "It's too bad we didn't uncover some closer relatives from my parent's siblings."

"Sadly, Edward had died during World War 2 and Barbara and her husband Alan had moved to Australia and had three children there, all girls who probably married there as well," said Meg.

"Knowing what I do now, I could probably search the Australian records myself and maybe find out some more, maybe some cousins," offered Flynn. "But this …" he waved his hand that encompassed the entire chart before them, "is amazing!" He looked around the room and then deciding on an appropriate place, said, "I think it would look great over on that wall."

"I'm looking forward to the DNA results," said Flynn. "They may even show us some of your Australian cousins, Gran." Meg hoped so too, it would verify all the work that had been done, and even though Alice was delighted with the findings, Flynn also wanted that seal of approval from the test results.

Flynn suddenly bounded from his chair. "Well, this calls for a celebratory drink," he said, and quickly went out the library door. In moments, he was back with a tray, carrying three glasses and a bottle of sparkling wine under his arm. "I bought this on my way from the airport. I had a feeling we would be toasting something special."

He popped the cork, carefully angling the bottle so it didn't overflow from the pressure. Then one by one filled their glasses and handed one to each of the women. Then, lifting his own in a toast, he said, "To family!"

"To family," echoed Alice and Meg.

Chapter 9

The sun was just above the horizon when they reached the pond. They sat together on a bench by the edge of the grassy slope watching, hoping to see some of the koi that inhabited the waters.

"This is nice," said Meg. "I love this time of day. The light has a yellow hue that gives things a different look."

Flynn sat back on the bench and looked up at the tree tops, considering this. "True, I've taken photos at this time of day and it's neat how the camera perceives the light. Gives things almost the look of a painting."

A fish jumped close to where they were sitting, hoping to catch a fly hovering over the water. The splash caught their attention; the sound breaking the quiet of the park. "I enjoyed supper tonight, thank you."

"I don't come here a lot, just for special occasions. And today was a special occasion. Gran was so happy. I think it gave her something of a connection, that she wasn't alone in the world."

"I'm glad."

"I'll start on the Australian branch tomorrow." He looked at Meg and smiled fondly. "Thank you again for teaching me the ropes. I feel a lot more confident now in researching, I may even tackle my mother's side of the Flynn family."

That made Meg happy; that she had shared the love of genealogy. "Do you think you will be home for a while?"

He laughed at that. "I suppose that depends whether I answer the phone or not, hopefully I can enjoy a few days."

"What about you, what are you working on now?"

The fish jumped again and a young couple walking by stopped and admired the small waterfall that emptied into the pond, wondering if the fish would appear again.

"I am currently looking at the London records, trying to find a four-times great grandfather who emigrated to England from South Africa after the Boer War."

"That sounds interesting."

Meg laughed. "All genealogy hunts are interesting, that's why I love it."

The sky started to cloud over, soft and gray.

Flynn nodded in agreement. "You probably realize by now that I've caught the bug, thanks to you." He reached over and took her hand in his. "You know, just because you're working from home now, doesn't mean we can't see each other more."

"I'm counting on it." She smiled and gave his hand a squeeze. "Come to my place tomorrow. You can see the furniture Alice gave me. It was so kind of her. I'll make supper."

"I'd like that."

The interior of the house looked much different than the last time he had seen it; boxes of unpacked belongings strewn throughout and misplaced furniture moved as a mass to one side of the room to make space. "This is beautiful," he said. "Really, you've turned this into a cozy home. It's amazing how accessories can tie everything together." Above the fireplace was a sixty-inch, flat-screen television. "When did you get that?"

"While you were away. Like it?"

He stood back by the couch admiring the new addition. "What's not to like."

"Do you notice anything familiar?"

Flynn looked around and noticed the antique clock on the wall that was centred above the sideboard. Meg had purchased a dark walnut dining room table that seemed to compliment the two older pieces. "Wow, I never thought they would look so great, especially with newer furniture."

"I love them. The desk is in my office, much nicer than my table." Then turning towards the kitchen, she said, "Come on, supper's almost ready."

Meg had set up a small dining area across from the kitchen, yet previously still part of it. Her new dining room furniture seemed too formal for just the two of them and she wanted something a bit more intimate. Everything finally unpacked, she had arranged some of her good dishes and cutlery for the occasion, augmented by a few of Alice's linens.

He could smell the food cooking, and knew by the aroma that Meg had gone to the trouble of making his favourite dish.

"I can't wait."

He swirled the last piece of Yorkshire pudding in the remaining puddle of gravy. The puddings had been cooking in a jumbo muffin pan, much like most he'd had, but these were much better. "How did you get them crispy on the outside and so moist on the inside. Most of the ones I've had are just dry."

"It's a secret" she said, smiling, "but I'll tell you. The batter has to rest before baking, a day at least."

"Really?" He looked a her puzzled. "How does that make any difference?"

Meg laughed softly. "I have no idea, but it works."

"I'll say it does. That's the best Yorkshire pudding I've ever had."

Meg flipped through her movie collection: a binder of more than three hundred films that she'd collected over many years, specializing in films from the 1930s, '40s and '50s. "Western, science fiction, film noir or comedy?"

Flynn leaned back on the couch, contemplating. "What, no romance?"

She smiled shyly. "I have a few. So, what will it be?"

"Science fiction, then."

"You'll like this one. *The Thing from Outer Space.* It's a cult classic."

For the next hour and a half, they sat together sipping the wine Flynn had brought and enjoying the film she'd chosen.

"Isn't that Matt Dillon from the Gunsmoke TV series," he asked, finally remembering where he'd seen the actor that played the monster.

"Yes." Meg paused the movie. "One of two science fiction films he was in, although he is mostly known for his westerns. How about some dessert?"

"Sure, I'd love some." He gave her a look that suggested something other than confections.

She smiled at his attempt at romance. "I'm afraid all I have for *now* is chocolate cupcakes."

It had arrived in the late afternoon; the proof that would confirm all the work they had done in searching for Alice's family. Nervous apprehension gave way to hopeful expectation as Meg opened up the package sent by the DNA research department of the genealogy site they had chosen to use.

Flynn and Alice sat with her in their office— now formally returned to its former name; library— as Meg printed the results quickly, hoping to find the evidence that would validate their work, then scanned the pages.

"Oh, no," said Meg. "There must be a mistake," she said almost to herself. She glanced at Flynn. "This doesn't make any sense." She hadn't heard of mistakes being made when it came to DNA results but certainly mistakes could be made even if only in a small percentage of tests. This had to be in that group because what she saw in front of her contradicted everything they had done in the last few weeks.

She handed the report to Flynn, the problem of questionable results showing in her face. "We will need to check the site for the copy of the results as well, just to double check."

Flynn was silent as he looked at the results, then scanned the pages for the familial results thinking that Meg's reaction was because none had been found. That would be a great disappointment to his grandmother.

"What does this mean?" he asked, as he folded back the page and pointed to what the document stated. "I don't understand."

Meg looked at Alice, then at Flynn. "It means that Alice has a male sibling, a brother living in Britain. It also shows further relatives; distant nieces and nephews, all living in the United Kingdom." Alice stared at her in disbelief. She could only imagine what Alice could be thinking. The only thing she could think of to explain the results, was that William Carter had sired other children during the war while he was serving in the army.

Alice was quiet for a few minutes taking in what the report had produced. "How can that be?" asked Alice. "I was their only child. No one ever spoke of other children."

"Maybe they didn't know," suggested Flynn, attempting to give William some slack. "It was war time after all. I mean, maybe William had a war time romance and never knew he had another child."

"That's the only thing that makes sense," added Meg.

"Are there any relatives for Canada?" asked Alice, sounding confused. "I mean there must be some nieces or nephews or hopefully even cousins from my parents, in Canada. What about some cousins in Australia?"

Meg nodded in agreement. "You would think so, but no, no one else but these people in Britain, which I agree is strange as well. There might be a mistake somewhere. But remember too, the site only shows people who have, like yourself, had their DNA analyzed and made it public." Flynn handed her the results and she looked at the matches again. "I know there might be a half of a percent chance that they might have made an error, but that still means ninety-nine percent of the results are accurate. I do know that usually when they match you with a brother, father, sister, half-sibling, first cousin, or second cousin, that it is considered a definite match. The further away, such as third cousins or fourth cousins, you might not match because you only share a small percentage of your DNA with them." She pointed to the main name that had put the results in question –Harold Fernsby. "But brother? That's pretty definite."

Flynn had sat down beside his grandmother and now took her hand in his, giving it a slight squeeze in reassurance. She smiled back at him, the look of disappointment still showing on her face.

"Are we allowed to contact this Harold Fernsby and ask him questions? Maybe he has family connections that are different from this one."

"We would have to go on the genealogical site and message him, and if he's a sibling and our theory is correct, he would be two to five years younger than Alice, so let's try. We should also check to see if his family tree is on the site too; whether it can be viewed or whether it's private."

Meg set up the site and found the matches for Alice, including Harold Fernsby, who, by the location map lived in London. "We click here to send a message to Harold."

"What should we say?" asked Alice.

"I suppose we say that you just got your results back and it shows him as your brother. We think it might be an error and ask if he has any knowledge of your parents; William and Anne Carter."

"How long do you think it will take for him to reply?" asked Flynn.

"Hard to say. I suppose it depends if he is still using that site and how often he checks his messages. Remember, we don't know how long ago he had his DNA test. I believe the site adds matches as they are revealed by the testing, but I'm not sure how often and whether they do that for a person who no longer has a subscription. All we can do is try."

"I suppose too, we could check the British directory and look for the name Harold Fernsby in London. If we get a few, maybe we could just phone some."

Alice's eyes lit up at that. "Can you imagine, if he actually is my brother. I wonder what he would think; suddenly hearing from a sister in Canada." The thought of a brother now, no longer disconcerting.

An hour later, they had messaged Harold Fernsby, giving the information they had for Alice and requesting information he might have regarding the results she had been given. All they could do now is wait for a reply.

Flynn returned the hammer and leftover screws to his tool pouch. He'd brought several necessary items for hanging various items to the walls Meg had selected. It had taken a few hours to hang up paintings, shelves and clocks, and now he stood on her deck after enjoying a well-deserved lunch.

"I love your new place." Flynn looked at her yard from the wooden deck. It had been a well-maintained garden overlooking a small water feature with falls, that sat unused at the moment.

"I think you did well, buying this place; it's a beautiful vintage home, on a cul-de-sac, with wide lot, fenced yard and fire pit."

Meg joined him on the deck, and offered him a glass of white wine. "I'm enjoying the house so far; I love the trees. The basement isn't that high

101

but it's dry and good for storage. The house is just the right size."

He took the proffered glass. "Thanks, and for lunch too. I didn't realize you were such a great cook."

She smiled. "I have a few favourite dishes that I like to make." She sat down at the small bistro table at the end of the deck. "I appreciate your help with the wall hangings."

He joined her and took a sip of the wine, and nodded its approval.

"Have you heard back from Harold Fernsby yet?" she asked.

"Not yet, I'm trying to keep Gran from thinking too much about it by sharing other facts that are on the computer program you gave me. She was very interested in the Mohawk connection. So, that seems to be working for the time being, but I know she must be thinking about her 'brother' when I'm not around. I hope he replies soon."

"Me too, but for now, let's think about other things."

He looked into Meg's eyes, then took her hand in his, and drew her close, then smiled. "I think I can come up with a few things."

Chapter 10

It was almost two weeks later that they had a response from their message to Harold Fernsby. Meg had stopped by to visit Alice, and while there, she and Flynn checked the genealogy site to see if there were any messages. With all the disappointing lack of responses Alice had attended over the last week, there was little expectation once Flynn had turned on his computer and opened up the site that contained Alice's information.

It felt strange sitting next to him again in their office. So much had happened since she had first met him. Flynn had kept his equipment there and would for the remainder of the summer before returning to work. Flynn had been called away only twice since his trip to Iroquois Falls and each time, for only a day or two. He'd spent the remainder of his time tending Alice's gardens, repairing and painting anything that needed repairing or painting, and many of his evenings with Meg.

Today though, she had spent most of the day with Alice, going over the ancestors on her chart, sharing time as the two went shopping in the town, and chatting about Flynn while they did so. The time out had tired Alice so she had retired for an afternoon nap shortly after their return.

Meg had joined Flynn, together with a box from the bakery. She set the box down along with two dessert plates from the kitchen. Flynn looked at the box and a smile came over his face. "Chocolate cupcakes?"

Meg smiled, and opened the box revealing four cupcakes, then set out one for each of them. She looked at the page that had just come on the screen after Flynn had put in Alice's password. The message box was checked and a sudden surge of excitement passed through her. Harold Fernsby had responded to their inquiry.

It was short and simply said, *"Thank you for your inquiry. My father has been waiting years to find you. I am his daughter, Alicia, I will get back to you shortly."*

She gave Flynn's arm a squeeze, a sudden chill came over her. "Oh, Flynn."

"This is wonderful!" said Flynn, happy with a final response, yet puzzled. "But on the other hand, now I'm very confused."

"I suppose the only scenario that makes sense is the wartime romance."

"True," agreed Flynn. "I suppose too, we will have to wait for her to get back to us, but ..." he smiled at their news, "Gran, will be so happy. I think she's gotten over the idea that her father had an affair, and was hoping she would hear from her brother."

"All those years alone, and now finding a brother," said Meg.

He picked up a cupcake and took a large bite. "Hmmmmm."

Meg laughed at his exaggerated enjoyment.

Meg arrived just after four o'clock, her researching done for the day. She'd gone back the requested number of generations for her new client, and actually found the records she was looking for without too much difficulty. There was one that was misspelled in the transcriptions as Springett instead of Springate that gave her a bit of a twist, but the ages and the birth records of the children matched the census records for the time, so it was fairly obvious that there had been a spelling issue on the part of the registrar. She was use to that, local dialects being what they were in Britain.

The gate to the Williams' residence had been left open for her as usual but there was another unfamiliar vehicle parked in her usual space, so she parked behind Flynn's car and getting out, she looked for Flynn at the front door. Instead, she saw Martha waiting for her. "They are in the back garden, Miss," she said. "They have been waiting for you, Alice is most excited."

Intrigued by this, she wondered why they weren't in the office room, ready to check the message that Flynn had telephoned her about, but said they would wait until they could read it together.

Meg followed Martha down the hallway that led to the back door of the house off the kitchen. Alice was seated at the garden bench opposite Flynn and another young man. There was a drawing over which they were both looking at and she advanced as Alice waved her over. "Isn't this wonderful," she said. "After all these years, to finally have some French doors off of the library. No more going through the kitchen."

Flynn greeted her with a warm embrace then introduced her to their contractor Ralph Comer. "I thought more about your suggestion," said Flynn. "Gran and I both agreed a door is just the thing we need for this end of the house."

"And," added Alice, "we can incorporate the original glass windows of the house into the doors."

Meg glanced at Flynn, and he smiled. Custom doors and construction would be very expensive, she thought. "My birthday gift to Gran," he said, as if reading her mind, then to the contractor, "Everything looks great Ralph. I think we can carry on with the project. You have all the measurements now, and the glass panels are by the garage." Meg glanced at the library wall and saw pressed-board; wooden sheets where the bevelled windows used to be.

The contractor nodded his farewell to everyone. "I'll call you when they are ready to install. It shouldn't take long."

Meg sat next to Alice on the bench under the maple tree. "That's exciting news. It's going to look beautiful."

"I think so too," said Alice. "Did Flynn tell you we got another message from Harold?"

"Yes, I can't wait to see it."

Flynn returned from seeing the contractor out and smiled seeing Meg and Alice together. He took up a chair opposite them. "There was a new message today, as I told you. We thought it would be nice to read it together."

"I'm glad. It sort of puts the end to the search and a new beginning for you, having a new family to get to know." She patted Alice's hand in support.

"Let's find out, shall we?" He helped Alice to her feet and together Meg and Flynn escorted her back to the library. The computer was already set up and ready to open up the new message.

"My dear sister," it started. *"You have no idea how long I have been wanting to say that. It's been eighty-three years since I last saw you, shortly after our parents sent me north for safety and they took you away to stay with a school friend of mother's. I was six when our parents died and had no way to find you until many years later. By that time, it was too late. I sit here with my daughter, Alicia Holmes; she is named after you.*"

The message was taken up after this by his daughter. She stressed the health of the eighty-eight-year-old who had been living with her for the past five years. He suffered from heart issues and she was afraid the stress and excitement at finding his sister might be too much for him at the moment. She suggested a possible video phone call or a Skype call. At the end she had left her phone number and internet links.

" 'Your parents'? " said Flynn. "What did he mean by parents?" He passed a look of bewilderment in their direction. "Now, I'm really confused."

Meg wasn't sure what to say. It seemed now that there must have been a mistake, yet how did he know Alice's name?

"My parents?" asked Alice. "How can that be?"

"And he's older than you, Gran, by three or four years," Flynn pointed out, in effect negating their war-time affair scenario.

"Why did they send the children away?" asked Alice.

Meg continued staring at the message, looking for any small details that could make sense of all this. "The war. Many British families sent their children to safety, anticipating possible bombing by the Germans. The government even had a plan to send children throughout the commonwealth as well as the United States for safety. Many children never came back to Britain."

"Do you think Gran might have been one of those children?" Flynn's grandmother looked at him then, her face showing the confusion, they both felt.

"Why don't we call them," suggested Alice. "We could ask more questions."

"True," said Meg. "They're six hours ahead of us, so it's a bit late now. Why don't we call tomorrow. In the mean time, Flynn and I can start to figure out what path to take from here in respect to searching.

Martha stood at the library door and knocked gently. "Supper's ready."

"Thanks, Martha. We'll be right there," said Flynn. He folded down the lid of his laptop, preparing to finish for the day. Once on their own, they would write down all the questions this revelation had implied.

Supper was unusually quiet after Alice had confided in Martha about her new found 'brother'.

Martha was at a loss for words, then voiced— what the rest at the table were thinking—out loud. "Do you think it could possibly be true?"

Alice had given her a look that said clearly that she didn't know.

"Hopefully we'll learn more once we actually have a conversation with them," answered Flynn.

Tomorrow found the three of them in the library at eleven o'clock. Meg searched for the information Harold's daughter had given them and found her available on Skype—hopefully awaiting their call.

Hesitantly she pressed the video button, the beeping sound calling the person at the other end. A moment later it was answered by a beautiful woman, perhaps in her late fifties.

"Hallo," she said, smiling.

"Hello, from Canada," said Flynn. "My grandmother Alice, is here too."

"I've been hoping you would call today. My father is here with me," she said.

Flynn got up and moved Alice's chair in front of the screen, then moved her chair back a bit so the people on the other end, could see her better.

The British Alicia turned her computer also so her father could be seen on their screen.

His voice was soft, filled with emotion. "Alice," he said. "I have been waiting for so long." His voice choked a bit then he regained his composure. "How have you been all these years?" There were tears in his eyes reflected in Alice's own eyes. He had the same blue eyes as she.

Alice cleared her throat, then spoke to her brother, if he was indeed her brother, for the first time. "I have had a good life, but a lonely one," she started, as tears filled her eyes. "I never knew I might have a brother, but at the same time I am confused as to the circumstances. My parents are William and Anne Carter, so I don't understand how you think they are not." Meg noticed that Alice had now accepted the name changes of her parents.

At that, Harold Fernsby started to cry. His daughter took over the screen, she knew the story so well after growing up with it for so many years. "Apparently in 1939 your parents had a new baby girl. It was difficult for your mother, a newborn and a toddler to care for. She had a close, friend who offered to take you temporarily, giving your mother a break. Once the war broke out in September, your parents were glad she had done this because the bombings started shortly after that. My father was sent to a shelter in the north with other children and your parents stayed in London with your mother's parents. A bomb fell directly on their home and they, with your little sister were killed instantly. My father was sent to a home for children later, but never forgot you."

A look of disbelief came over Alice. All that she had known, grew up believing, was suddenly gone, if what Harold's daughter said was true. "What were their names?" she asked.

"Walter and Emily Fernsby," Harold replied. "Our sister was Angela." He'd composed himself now, eager to make her understand.

Flynn had been silent during this but suddenly had a question. He introduced himself then asked, "Is Alicia your only child?"

Harold smiled at this. "Your Alice, has a niece named Alicia," he nodded towards his daughter. "And, a nephew Walter. Walter has two boys and he lives in Liverpool."

Alice looked into his eyes feeling his emotion. "I have one son; Richard, and two grandchildren; Flynn and Ann," she said. "My life has been full, but missing a connection, a connection I realize now, to my people. I always thought I knew who I was, but often wondered why I had no relatives growing up. It was just me and my … parents."

"I'm sorry … if I have turned your world upside down," he said. "It's just that I'm so glad to have found you. I took the genealogy DNA test many years ago hoping one day you might too, and now what I had hoped for has happened."

He sighed, but continued, "I will have Alicia send you any documents and photos that might be of an interest to your family." He coughed and sat back from the computer.

His daughter took over then. "I'm sorry, we will have to continue again another day. I will send you whatever I have on the family. Farewell Auntie."

The connection was terminated, leaving Alice, Flynn and Meg dumbfounded.

What had just happened. In one Skype call Alice's world had changed. '*Auntie.*' But was it all true?

Meg glanced at the family tree chart Flynn had pinned to one of the walls of the library, the dotted lines between the Carters and Alice, still not proven, and now possibly no longer relevant, and all the joy Alice had experienced in discovering her family—gone, then she looked at Flynn. There were so many questions and no one left to ask.

How did Alice get to Canada or was she indeed the same child?

Could the DNA have mixed up 2 people named Alice?

Who was the friend that took Alice?

And if true, had William and Anne Carter just kept Alice with no regard for her possible family in Britain?

Had they tried to find her parents after the war? Is what Harold Fernsby told them true, or did he confuse William and Anne's Alice with his sister?

What should they do now?

The only way, she thought, was to find some proof that Alice, a year old, had come to Canada sometime between 1939 and 1941.

Alicia Holmes had sent the documents her father had promised the next day. Unfortunately, they were all related to his immediate family, and although nice for Alice to have; didn't shed any further light on his parents.

"Maybe the new caregiver for Alice was British and they just moved to the country," suggested Flynn.

"Maybe. I think for us to move forward we will have to look for Alice on a ship leaving from Britain for those years. We need to check for Anne Carter as well," said Meg, "just in case she went to them and brought Alice back."

She made some notes for this approach before continuing. "We have two different scenarios to consider. One—that Harold is correct and somehow his sister came to Canada, or two— and with the DNA, less likely—that William and Anne Carter are your grandmother's actual parents. We haven't found a birth record on-line, so it leaves us with option one to figure out."

Flynn nodded. "So, if option one is correct, we need to find Harold's actual sister and see what happened to her and then find some proof of her leaving Britain."

"That's about it, and if we find her still in Britain it will show she isn't your grandmother. But a problem we might have, is that he doesn't know who took his sister. If they 'adopted Alice' she may be listed under a different last name; the enumerator thinking she was actually the family's child, or worse still; even her first name, which I hope isn't the case."

It was early still, so they decided to begin a new search. Alice had been visibly upset with the news her 'brother' had given her and had decided not to question a new search and leave things up to Meg and Flynn to figure it out.

"Use this site," said Meg. "Look for any name close to Fernsby leaving Britain, as well as anyone named Carter." She checked on the site Flynn would use. "I think too, maybe we should check Hughes as well. I'll work on anyone named Alice, aged one to ten, leaving Britain."

He reached over and took her hand, giving it a squeeze. "Thank you for helping with this. I know you have other clients right now."

She returned the squeeze, understanding. "I wouldn't feel right taking my commission for something that turned out to be wrong."

He nodded, in approval. "Let's hope we find something."

The sun had come around to the garden side of the house now, but wooden sheets over the windows didn't have shimmering bevels that danced as they had so many days before.

"I'm done," said Flynn. "So far I found one Fernsby, an Augusta aged fifty-five and two

Carters, both men who had wives and children with them, and no Hughes."

"I haven't done much better. I've searched eighty-one pages and have fourteen Alices, and as you found, all with parents and siblings, and none with relevant last names."

He leaned back in his chair, considering. "Well, that would seem that Alice didn't come to Canada."

"It would seem so, but we have to consider too, that we might be missing some records; not every site has everything, and not everything has been transcribed."

"It's getting late, why don't we take a break and maybe go for a walk before supper."

"Good idea, I think I need a break, now."

Chapter 11

They sat on one of the small, wooden benches that lined both sides of the main street providing respite for weary shoppers.

Flynn took another bite of the chocolate cupcake he had just purchased in the bakery opposite them.

Meg smiled and glanced at the street clock. "Aren't you afraid that will spoil your supper."

"No," he said, then took the last bite. He smiled while he finished chewing then said, "because I told Martha we weren't staying in for supper tonight."

He tossed the paper wrapper in the trash bin next to the bench. "I've been thinking, could Alice have been brought to Canada after the war?" suggested Flynn.

"Maybe, but I don't think so, she would have been, seven or eight, old enough to remember a trip like that."

"So, where does that leave us?"

"We now continue to look for Harold's sister Alice Fernsby. It would be a bit easier if he had definite dates. There were no census records during the war but there was the 1939 registry. We look for the family and see if we can find her with her parents in London."

"That's one way to see if she actually existed."

"Yes, but the problem is, when the directory was taken. It was done September 29, 1939, after war was declared. We might find Harold's parents, but it's a long shot if we find Alice on it. It's worth the search though."

"Come on." Flynn took her hand and pulled her to him as he stood. "I know a great place to have supper, just around the corner. He gave her a quick hug." A young couple passed by, giving them a knowing look, and smiled.

"Hmmm. I wonder if they have fish and chips there?" said Meg.

"That, or roast beef with gravy and mashed potatoes. Oh, and Yorkshire pudding." Meg laughed and entwined her arm in his as they walked down the street towards their favourite go-to place for supper. She loved the feel of him, as they walked, and wondered where their relationship would go, once he went back to work and her research for Alice was finally completed. She hoped it would continue for the long term, but time would tell.

"Do you know that the secret to a good Yorkshire pudding is allowing it to rest over night, before cooking?"

That made Meg laugh and they walked on, momentarily forgetting their lost child dilemma.

<hr/>

"There, found them."

Flynn leaned over to look at Meg's screen. He read the names as she spoke them.

"Walter and Emily Fernsby, living on Danbrook Road, Wandsworth, London. Harold (son implied), born December 1934, single, at school.

Angela (daughter implied), born April 1939, infant."

Flynn read the results again. These people were indeed Harold's family, but no proof though of his sister Alice. "So, it would seem that Alice has gone already with her mother's friend."

"It looks that way. Let's try plugging in Alice's name and birth year and see if anything comes up in Britain."

A thought occurred to Flynn. "Did Canada have a 1939 registry?"

"We had something similar, called the National Resources Mobilization Act, 1940, the compulsory registration of all persons, 16 years of age or older, between 1940 and 1946. This allowed the government to identify military and labour resources that could be mobilized in fighting the war, but like a lot of records in Canada, you can only access them if you have proof a person has been dead for at least 20 years." She gave him a look. "Good old 'Privacy Act'."

Flynn smiled at that. "So, we have to either find our Alice on a boat or plane coming to Canada, or find Harold's sister still somewhere in Britain during the years our Alice was here in Canada, in order to prove anything."

"Exactly, except for the plane part. Plane records weren't kept for more than thirty days back then, if at all." Meg sat back and studied her notes from the morning. "Hmmm. If she came to Canada around 1939 or 1940, her name would have been Alice Fernsby, but if she stayed in Britain, her name might be listed as Fernsby or as an implied daughter of the caregiver who had her."

"And we don't know who that was."

"Right. There might be some other sources we could check after, like newspaper obituaries for Harold's parents. It might mention the children. I wish there were school records for Emily Fernsby we could check, although like here, if any did exist, they'd be few and far between, if at all.

"Don't tell me … privacy rules."

Meg laughed at that. "Yes, requests for access to school records 100 years old or less must be submitted in writing to the Information and Privacy Unit of the Archives of Ontario," she quoted, "and I'm sure Britain has similar privacy rules. It doesn't mean it's not something we could try later once we have a plausible reason to try."

"If our Alice and Harold's are the same, then maybe there might be a class yearbook somewhere with Emily and Anne's names in it," suggested Flynn.

"We just have to connect the two together some how. It wouldn't be proof, but there would be enough circumstantial evidence to give it plausibility. Might as well get started. Which do you want to try?"

"I seemed to have good luck with newspapers before, and I'm familiar with that site so I'll try that first. If there is an obituary it should be in a London newspaper."

Ralph showed up early in the afternoon, ready to install whatever structure was necessary to support the two new doors that sat wrapped up on their sides, leaning against the bench.

"Can I give you a hand," asked Flynn.

"Thanks, Joe's out by the truck getting the tools but with an extra pair of hands, this won't take long."

Flynn glanced at the wrapped doors. "I'm surprised you finished so quickly."

"We had the doors, being a standard size, only had to cut them so the windows would fit."

Meg covered over their computers and printer in case of dust that might result from their installation, then obligingly left the men to their work and joined Alice in the living room. She was having an afternoon cup of tea and some almond biscuits. Martha sat in a small chair, a basket of yarns in complementary colours by her chair leg. She sat knitting as Meg came through, into the room.

"Come, join us, dear," suggested Alice.

Meg took a place next to Alice. "They're working on your doors now," said Meg, "Flynn is helping them."

"Good." She patted Meg's knee. "It gives us some time to chat."

Meg could only imagine how Alice must be feeling, discovering that your parents were not your parents; she'd had a difficult time with Steven Hughes being William Carter. Was Alice secretly wishing that she was Harold's sister or that there had been some mistake, something that would hold the world she'd know for eighty-four years, together?

Alice smiled kindly at Meg, as Martha gave her a sideways glance. They'd must have been talking about her. "How are you and Flynn getting along?" she asked softly, her look, implying a confidence between the three of them.

"Quite well, actually. We are checking newspapers, and the 1939 registry for any sign of… —*she couldn't say* Alice, *not with Flynn's grandmother in doubt of everything right now*—of Harold's sister living in England."

Alice passed Meg a cup of tea that she'd poured, then waited as Meg added milk and sugar to the contents of the china cup. She gave her fellow conspirator a questioning look. "What I meant, is, how is your relationship going?"

Meg felt her face flush and noticed Martha pause in her knitting waiting for her to answer. "Oh," said Meg. She glanced back to make sure no one was at the door to the living room, then she smiled. "I think it's coming along just fine. We seem to like each other and we get along well. I'm hoping it continues into something more."

Alice reached over and gave her hand a pat. "I'm so glad. I've been hoping Flynn would find a nice girl to get serious with."

She smiled at Alice's enthusiasm. Martha nodded in agreement, then resumed her knitting. "Well, we haven't quite reached that stage yet, time will tell I suppose." She took a sip of tea to avoid having to continue on the subject of Flynn and their relationship, realizing now that they did have a relationship, even though she wasn't really sure what it was. Instead, she changed the subject to the library doors. "It will be so nice for you to be able to go out into the garden from the library, instead of walking around to the other side of the house."

"I think so too," said Alice. I really do love that room but it felt so isolated with only the one door to the hallway, that I didn't use it often, perhaps now I will."

They heard a shout and a resulting curse come from the direction of the library, "Uh—oh," said Meg. "Sounds as if someone put their finger where a nail should have been."

"I'll check." She left the two women, while she went to check on a possible injury. She found Flynn holding one of the doors with a free hand while shaking the other as if trying to get the circulation back in it. Ralph and Joe were measuring the level of the frame and shimming where necessary as they attached the hinges.

Flynn smiled with a wince when he saw her. "Hammer-one, Flynn-zero."

"My fault," said Ralph. "The door slipped." She went over to check while Flynn was still holding the door.

"It's not too bad, but the nail will probably turn black. Maybe an icepack will help."

"You can let go now Flynn," said Ralph. "We can take it from here."

Flynn nodded and followed Meg to the kitchen for some ice.

Harold's daughter had sent an email. Eager to read it, Meg and Flynn had waited for Alice to join them. Meg opened the message; it included an attachment as well.

"Dear Auntie," it started. *"It's so nice to say that to you. I have gone through my father's records and found this picture. I thought you might like to see it. My father's aunt—having found him years later after the war—sent this to him. She didn't know where he had gone after his parents were killed and didn't know where to find him. He was married when she finally saw his name in the newspapers celebrating his marriage. This is a wedding picture of his parents' wedding in 1934, that she had; my grand parents. She thought my father would like to have it as he had nothing left after the house was destroyed. I thought this would help to create a connection for you. My father is so happy. I can't tell you what this means to us. There wasn't a time I remember when he didn't talk about you."* It was signed, *"Happily, your niece, Alicia."*

Meg noticed Alice's eyes glisten with repressed tears. "Let's make a print of this," she suggested.

Flynn gave his grandmother's shoulders a hug in support. "What are you thinking?"

"She looks so much like me when I was her age, at my wedding." Alice was visibly upset; the reality that this scenario was now possible. She put her hand on Flynn's seeking some kind of logical explanation. "Do you think this is really true?"

Flynn stared at the picture. He hadn't known his grandmother when she was young, obviously, and didn't readily see a resemblance. "I don't know," said Flynn. "Do you have any pictures of yourself at her age?"

"Yes, somewhere, I'll ask Martha." She looked a bit flustered as if trying to remember where she had put her family photos, and worried at the same time, because she didn't know.

Meg printed two high-resolution copies of the picture, while Alice went to hunt for her photographs.

Flynn stood by Meg at the printer, his arm around her. "What do you think?" he asked. The photo slowly progressed through the printer and finally sat on top of the printer ready to view.

"I don't know." Meg picked up the picture of the happy couple. "The bride and groom in the foreground look good and their faces are sharp, but the bridal party behind are a bit out of focus."

Just as the second photograph appeared from the machine, Alice and Martha came through the door, album in hand.

"Martha found my wedding album for me," said Alice. They placed the album on the table then turned to the page that showed Alice with her new husband—Richard Williams. Every one crowded around as Meg put the printed picture next to the couple in the album.

"Oh, my goodness," said Martha. "They could be sisters."

It was true. The two brides looked to be the same person; the resemblance was remarkable.

Alice stared at the pictures. "It must be true," she said, in a voice barely audible.

Martha moved to put her arm around her friend. "There must be some logical explanation."

Flynn gave Meg a look of bewilderment. This, with the DNA report seemed to solidify Harold's claim, but how. There had to be a connection between Emily Fernsby and Anne Carter. It would take some time to go through more records and figure it out.

Flynn's fear was that they wouldn't be able to.

Meg stared at the picture in front of them. "We'll have to get creative."

"What about newspapers?" suggested Flynn. "This picture has no names attached to it other than a hand written sentence below it about Walter Fernsby's marriage. It doesn't even mention the bride's name. Don't they usually have the names of everyone in a picture when they publish it?"

"Good thinking." Meg considered the photograph she held now. "I would have thought so, but maybe not. It does look, though, as if the aunt just cut out the picture and pasted it in an album of some kind. You can still see a bit of the gray, card-stock paper around the edges. The only way to find out is to find the original page and any article that might have gone with it."

Flynn nodded in agreement. "Since I now have my own subscription to the newspaper site you introduced me to, I think I can tackle that."

"I think I will find Emily's maiden name. If she was a friend of Anne Ramsey's, then she might have gone to school in Canada, so again passenger lists might yield something ... it's a long shot."

They sat quietly for the next half hour, each immersed in their respective search.

"I found her. On Harold's civil registration birth record."

Flynn stopped for a moment. "Do they list the mother's name?"

"Yes, as of 1911 they started to list the 'maiden' name of the mother in the records." She printed out the record. "Here, Harold Fernsby and his mother's maiden name is Emily Robson."

"That's great, so now where from here?"

Meg leaned over to see what Flynn had found. "So, then I'll check for passenger lists for an Emily Robson, and see if I can find her coming to Canada, you never know, we might find something."

"Any luck with the newspaper yet?"

"No, not yet. I have their marriage date from the Civil Registration. It's just trying to find the right newspaper."

Meg, sighed, annoyed at herself. "You know, while we've been focused on Harold as Alice's brother, being such a shock to all of us that he was, we've overlooked the distant relatives on the DNA test. Maybe they are grandchildren of Walter or Emily's siblings. Maybe someone knows something that might help us figure this out."

Flynn nodded in agreement. "It's worth a try. Let's check and see if we can contact them."

Meg was already back on the site that gave the results for Alice and focused now on any other blood relative the test found. "The problem is that some of these names might be from people who are quite old already and maybe don't check this site any longer, or they might be too young to know anything about Alice."

Flynn rolled his chair closer to Meg so he could view the screen.

"Here, a Thomas Gilchrist, from Kent," she said. "And there are two others; a Barbara Hanson, from Devon and an Ivy Carlisle from London."

"Wait a minute!" said Meg. "We've overlooked someone." She opened up another window and went back to the message Alicia had sent regarding the wedding photograph. "How could I have been so stupid." She ran her hand across her face in frustration.

Flynn reread the message. "It's been emotional for all of us, and especially for Gran. You can't help but be distracted." He looked at the screen then turned to Meg his eyebrows raised in question.

"His aunt," said Meg. "That implies she was related to either Walter or Emily. We can ask Alicia who she was and maybe Harold learned more about her family since he got the photo."

She flipped back to the DNA site. "Maybe one of these is related to her and maybe there is some more information we can find out from them."

With a new direction now to follow, they took time to send a message to each of the three. Now it would just take some time for them to answer.

Then they messaged Alicia and asked her more about the mysterious aunt.

"Now all we can do is wait," said Meg.

"Well, I don't know about you, but I need a drink."

He pushed his chair back enough to stand up and offered Meg his hand. "Come on."

Chapter 12

They walked down the street towards the town. He stopped in front of a small pub; one she hadn't noticed before. Inside they were seated at a small wooden table near the front where large windows showed tourists and shoppers as they passed by.

"This is all so overwhelming. Let's take a break," said Flynn. "Maybe a day or so will give us a different perspective."

"Maybe, but my mind won't give it up as easily."

He nodded in agreement. "True, mine too, and I doubt Gran will stop thinking about it as well."

The waiter came back with their drink order and paused briefly in case they wanted to order something else.

The pub was interesting, rustic and made to seem a place of gathering as it might have been in the seventeenth century. Staff members, dressed in similar attire to represent the spirit of the times moved throughout the room bringing appreciative guests, their orders.

Meg looked at the mulled wine before her, served in a pewter mug, a slice of lemon floating on the surface. "I've never had this before." She took a cautious sip.

"It's usually a winter drink but it is delicious and too much trouble to make at home. Not sure what kind of red wine they use but I can taste one or two spices I recognize."

"Oh … it is good. I'm going to check out recipes."

September 1940, Ontario, Canada

It was just after eight o'clock. Anne finished putting the baby to bed then went to sit by the radio. News of the war was usually first on the CBC broadcast and she sat eagerly to hear of something that might give her hope as to the Canadians overseas, hoping she hadn't missed something important that might mention her husband's regiment, but instead came news of the German bombings of London. Nazi Germany had turned its wrath upon the citizens of London, indiscriminate and unrelenting, night after night the bombers flew over the homes of families, in neighbourhoods like hers.

The announcer paused in his distain of the cowardly act, to air a portion of Churchill's speech-

'Little does he know the spirit of the British nation, or the tough fibre of the Londoners, whose forbears played a leading part in the establishment of Parliamentary institutions and who have been bred to value freedom far above their lives. This wicked man, the repository and embodiment of many forms of soul-destroying hatred, this monstrous product of former wrongs and shame, has now resolved to try to break our famous island race by a process of indiscriminate slaughter and destruction.

What he has done is to kindle a fire in British hearts, here and all over the world, which will glow long after all traces of the conflagration he has caused in London have been removed.'

"We join the people of London in their resolve and we pray for the innocent lives that are enduring this unimaginable horror," the announcer concluded. The program continued with local news.

Once the news turned to the weather across Canada, Anne turned if off. She leaned back against her chair. William, she still thought of him as William even though the army had changed their identities. He'd left in December of last year for the island that was now being bombed. She prayed that he was safe and was somewhere other than London.

Like many of the soldier's wives she felt a deep loneliness, and wished she could just telephone her father and her close friends from a year ago, but that would endanger herself and them, not to mention baby Alice. The threats had been real and if the dead man's friends knew where they now were, there would be reprisals, against her and her family. William knew that to be true as well, and had, like herself, resisted the urge to send word after the trial had ended.

They had each sent a letter to their respective parents—her mother had been alive then—and briefly explained they must go away, for their own safety as well as theirs, to have no more contact with family members or friends. Both families had known about William's part in the saboteur's trial and had feared for them; knowing the threats they'd received. Her father had

131

understood. Maybe one day they could resume their old life but not now.

William's picture sat on the flat top of the floor radio, a small oval-framed portrait of him, handsome in his uniform. She picked up the picture and held it to her. She closed her eyes and said a prayer for him and for the people of London.

2022 Niagara, Ontario, Canada

"Ok, we've looked for Alice coming to Canada—nothing. We've looked for Anne and Emily on passenger lists—nothing. Now, bearing in mind that lack of finding records isn't proof they don't exist, we are sort of at a standstill; unless we travel to Kew in Britain and look at actual records, or take another route."

Flynn had been nodding agreement as she listed their obstacles, but now he was curious as to what she was getting at. "So ... ?"

"We start over, we go lateral. There must be some connection between Emily and Anne; you just don't give your child to anyone. Maybe Harold had it wrong. Maybe there wasn't a school connection, which in one way would be good because the records are few, if at all for this time period. Maybe it was something else, so we start to broaden our search. We look into their parents, aunts and uncles, siblings for each of our families, and if that brings up nothing, we try to check on neighbours and see if there's a connection."

Encouraged once more, Flynn nodded, confirming this new approach.

"So, which one do I work on?"

Meg smiled at his eagerness, then laughed. "Your choice."

"I'll take William and Anne then."

"Right, then look to see what happened to Anne's sisters and William's brother and the sister that didn't go to Australia and I'll work on the Walter Fernsby and Emily families."

"Okay, start by checking for marriages, deaths, and residence. Then move on to the parents and aunts and uncles."

Flynn nodded in understanding. "We'll make note of any new surnames that are found through marriages for both Canadian and British families," she added.

By the third hour Flynn had finished with the William and Anne side of the family, in so far as the siblings went, helped along the way by Meg and his grandmother's earlier exploration into aunts and uncles. It had taken less time than he had expected.

He sat back and sighed, giving his eyes a rest, and yawned quietly. "I'm so tired. I'm glad I have an outdoor job."

Meg paused, making note of the page she was on before turning towards his computer. "What did you find out?"

Flynn turned to his notes, and flipping the pages in triumph, revealed his own sketch of a family tree, one each for William Carter and his wife Anne Ramsey.

"William's youngest sister Mary Carter, married a John Burton and I found them on the Toronto directories until 1949, then they must have moved, maybe to join her sister Barbara Hendricks in Australia" His brother Thomas was also in the army. I found his death record in the Canadian War Deaths records. He died in Italy, 1944.

Meg sat back and listened as Flynn added two more surnames to their list of hopeful connections— Burton and Hendricks.

"Well done," she said, actually impressed.

Flynn turned the page in his notebook. "On the Anne Ramsey side there were a few more siblings. She had two sisters and three brothers. You and Gran had already discovered the death of the one-year-old twins—David and Frank. Her other brother died in 1938. He was a boxer and died suddenly after his last fight. There was a newspaper article about him, discussing the fight with possible causes as to his death. He wasn't married. Anne's sister Sarah married a guy named Joe Milton in Toronto. I couldn't find anything about the eldest sister—Elizabeth. No marriage or death in Ontario. So, in all we have three surnames to watch out for— Milton, Hendricks and Burton."

Meg agreed. "We'll have to look into Elizabeth further. She may have also gone to Australia as there could be a connection with William's sister Mary."

There was a soft ding coming from Flynn's computer indicating an e-mail.

"It's from Alicia." He opened up his email page and clicked on her message.

"Hallo, cousin,

I spoke with my father and he is quite sure that the aunt who had sent him the picture of his parents wedding was his Aunt Calli on his father's side. I'm sorry he doesn't know more than that; she died shortly after sending it. I hope that helps in some way.

Talk soon, Alicia."

Quickly, Flynn wrote back a short thank you and let her know they would keep her apprised of any further findings.

"What do you think? Have you come across a Calli yet?"

Meg had looked puzzled at reading the e-mail. "No. Is Calli an actual name or a nick name?"

A shadow passed where the bevels normally danced across the long table. The door to the garden opened and Alice entered, smiling. "I love my new doors," she said, approaching the table. She looked at the window inserts from inside the room. "They are beautiful, Flynn. Thank you so much."

Meg got up from her chair and went to hug Alice. "I'd like to invite you and Flynn to my house for your birthday tomorrow," she said.

"I'd like that very much. That would give Martha an evening off too, which I'm sure she will appreciate."

"Your home is beautiful," said Alice. She approached the side board and her hand glided smoothly across the surface as a nostalgic look overtook her face, but just for a moment, and then was gone. "It looks beautiful here." She turned when the low sound of the clock's chime told of six o'clock. "And the clock!" She turned and gave Meg a warm hug. "I'm so glad they are here, being used again, being honoured here by their place of prominence."

For this special occasion Meg had set up her dining room table for the three of them, using some of Alice's linens in place of her own. She led the way to the back of the house, to the kitchen area and then to the back yard. "Flynn has promised to barbeque for us. Why don't you enjoy the garden, while I put the vegetables on, and Flynn can get the grill ready."

The air grew cooler after supper and the string of twinkle lights Meg had strung up the day before came on as the light faded from the yard. "Thank you for inviting us," said Alice. "The meal was delicious, and especially that beautiful birthday cake."

"I'm glad you enjoyed it."

"You got the water feature going," observed Flynn, the sound of gurgling water, audible from where he stood.

"I'd intended to help you with that."

Meg laughed. "That was kind of you but I do have a few skills. We had a pond at home with a similar set up. All I need now are few gold fish, or maybe I'll try a koi fish."

Meg noticed that Alice had hesitated to ask up to now, but seemed curious as to how their search was going, so she offered some of their results.

Flynn and I are looking into all of the aunts and uncles now on both sides of the ocean. We think there has to be some connection between Anne Carter and Emily Fernsby. Emily wouldn't have given her child to just anyone."

Alice considered that for a moment. "So, if I am Harold's sister, you think there should be a relative or close friend who brought me here?"

"Exactly, only we're hoping it's a relative which would be easier to find. We're checking all the marriages and making note of all the last names and then searching for passenger lists. Flynn's working on William and Anne and I'm looking into Emily and Walter's side. If we don't find anything there, then we go back to the grandparents and start again."

Alice shook her head slightly, trying to absorb all of this. "It seems like so much work."

"It's necessary," said Flynn, "If we want to find absolute proof. And we do," he added.

"Meg's good at this. We'll figure it out." He gave her hand an encouraging pat.

November 1940, Toronto, Ontario, Canada

Anne had saved the letter she had received until after Alice had retired for the night; she didn't want the child to see her crying while reading the words from her husband. She knew he had finally left Scotland and was due to head to the south of England, but when he would be sent to fight, she didn't know. It was November and the enemy continued to bomb London and other major industrial areas of England hoping to break the British people.

Like his previous letters he was unable to include any particulars about Army plans, regarding his future deployments, but rather, discussed things acceptable to the military censors. Without giving names or facts she knew what he was writing about.

My Dearest Anne,
I can't believe how fast the time has passed. It will be almost a year since I last saw you. I am well and I thank you for the package you sent on my birthday. The cake was delicious and I shared it with my close friends. Thank you too, for the cigarettes you sent me. I was able to trade them for delicacies which I gave to my host family. We don't realize how lucky we are in Canada. The people here have been on strict rationing since the start of the war. They have been great and have treated Ted and I as their own sons, sharing what little they have with us.

It saddens me to tell you that the family we care about that lived in London have died after a bomb fell on their home, there were no survivors. It leaves little Alice for us to care for now.

Buy something special for our girl at Christmas. I will try to write again before that.

I love you and I miss you,
Steve

Chapter 13

2022 Niagara, Ontario, Canada

It was almost one and there were still foggy patches in the lower areas of roads and fields on her drive to Alice's home. Today she would finish up the aunts and uncles on the Fernsby side—and there were a lot of them—then move on back to the next generation. There had to be a connection somewhere.

Their usual working space seemed warm and comfortable now to her, and she quickly set up her equipment next to Flynn who had been already working on finding the elusive sister of Anne Carter—Elizabeth Ramsey.

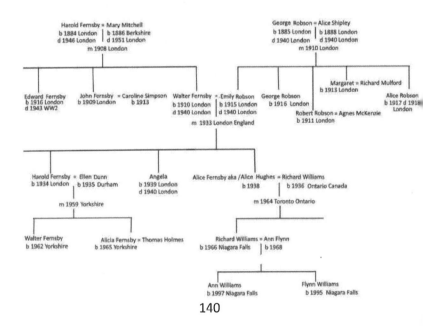

"Finally found her," said Flynn triumphantly.

"Good, where did she go?" said Meg as she sat down beside Flynn, the closeness to him still gave her a feeling of electrical twinges, and she smiled at his enthusiasm. "She went on vacation to France, and possibly other countries as well, but there's no way of knowing."

"Well. Last night I finally finished up the Fernsby siblings. It took a while." She opened her notebook to the rough chart she had made of the family. Walter had two brothers—Edward and John. Edward died in 1943, John married a girl named Caroline Simpson."

"So, there's another surname to add to our list."

"Yes, and a few more on Emily's side. Emily had two brothers and two sisters: George, Robert, Margaret and Alice. Alice died of the flu in 1918. Margaret married a man named Richard Mulford, George died in 1930 and Robert married a girl named Agnes McKenzie. Now we have Simpson, Mulford and McKenzie from the Emily's side."

Flynn sat back, considering where they go from here. "I don't recognize any names that match any from the Carter side."

"No, so we go back and check now for the any cousins, and we'll start on Anne and Emily's side first before moving on to the husband's cousins."

"Meanwhile my detective buddy, you will do what you are good at." Flynn raised a brow at that. "You will search for that wedding picture and see which names are mentioned. And, I'm hoping we find a connection there with someone."

He gave her a mock salute and opened up his notepad to a fresh page.

It was close to supper time and Flynn still hadn't found the wedding picture he'd been seeking. "Well, at least I know which newspapers don't have the picture," he said, and showed her the list of papers he had gone through all ready."

"I've made some progress," said Meg, "but I'm ready for a break."

"Good, I was hoping you would say that. I'm exhausted."

July 1944, Toronto, Canada

It was ten o'clock in the morning, a time that she would remember for the rest of her life, when the door bell rang. Anne handed Alice her rag doll and left to answer the door. A young man with a Canadian National Telegrams badge on his cap, stood behind the screen door, a solemn look on his face, and sad speculation in his eyes. He'd delivered these telegrams before and dreaded the reaction he might get from the woman before him, a small child clutching her dress, eyes wide.

He held out his hand and she hesitated just a moment before taking it and thanking the boy.

She opened it slowly dreading what it might say, hoping there was a mistake in the address. She read her name across the top and her address below it. Alice was tugging at her skirt and she took her hand. "Go play with dolly, dear, then we can have some cookies and milk."

Alice dutifully went to the kitchen, eager for her treat with mother.

'**IT IS WITH REGRET THAT WE INFORM YOU THAT ...**' She stopped and stared at his regimental number; not your husband but number. The tears started and she blinked them away and wiped her cheek with a free hand. '... **LIEUTENANT STEVEN HUGHES HAS BEEN OFFICIALLY REPORTED BY THE INTERNATIONAL RED CROSS QUOTING GERMAN INFORMATION TO HAVE BEEN TAKEN PRISONER JUNE 4 1944 AND IS NOW A PRISONER OF WAR STOP FURTHER INFORMATION TO FOLLOW** It was signed **DIRECTOR OF RECORDS**.'

Anne crushed the telegram to her chest. "Mummy, Mummy!"

2022 Niagara, Ontario, Canada

"How long will you be gone?"

"Just a few days," replied Flynn, as he checked the map he had for this particular project. I have to go to Nephton and check on a mine there." He laughed when he saw her mouth the name Nephton with a questioning look. "It's up near Peterborough, on Big Mountain Lake." She nodded accepting his explanation.

"Hey, why don't you come with me? I have a friend who has a lodge near by and I can get us a couple of rooms. Not sure what exactly; being the peak season but I'm sure he'll find something for us. He does have the internet, so you can relax a bit while you're working on research when I'm at the Peterborough office, then we can have some free time later."

There was nothing pressing at home, and a short vacation might be nice. "I'd like that, but we need to share the expenses. If you get the accommodations, then I pay for the gas there and back"

Flynn looked at her considering, knowing it was no use in arguing. "Deal. I'll call my friend Trevor and I'll pick you up at five a.m."

"Okay ..." she said, giving him a dubious look, wondering if he was serious. "I think I'll leave now, then, and go home and pack a few things ready, and hunt for my fishing rod and lures. Maybe we can go fishing, it's been several years since I've been, but I still have my equipment ... somewhere."

It was five minutes to five when Flynn pulled into her driveway. The morning dampness still clung to the grass and shrubs and the sun was just beyond the horizon; the light giving a grayness to the eastern sky. It took less than five minutes to pack her small suitcase, a cooler and fishing gear in the trunk, and then they were off.

By six-thirty they had reached as far as the Burlington Skyway. Traffic had begun to slow down as they approached Oakville. They'd stopped at a rest stop along the way and ate breakfast—shaved ham and Havarti cheese on a bun that Meg had

144

thought to pick up on her way home yesterday—
while watching other travellers come and go.

"I'm glad you thought of these," said Flynn,
finishing up his last bite of the bun. "And the coffee
too. It saves a lot of time waiting in line for a coffee
at the food court, especially at this time of day
when it will be very crowded."

"Crowded is right; there was a line up at the
washrooms too."

"Well, we're making good time now. We
should be there by nine."

By eight-forty they had reached their
destination with only minor delays due to road
repair.

Flynn pulled up to the main office, to check
in while Meg got out and looked around the lodge
facilities. Flynn had warned her that it wouldn't be
anything fancy. The cottages had originally been
built with fishermen in mind and compared to other
lodges and resorts in the area, accommodations
would be a bit primitive.

But being also one of the first camps set up
in this area, the lodge was situated on prime real
estate. The land, two hundred acres or more was
situated on a large peninsula; the docking area
protected on one side facing east, while the beach
area, now filled with happy families took up the
western side.

Flynn stood now on the office porch, with a
key in his hand, and he smiled at Meg as he
approached their car. "We're in luck, he has one
small cabin left we can have." Meg noticed he

didn't say cottage and wondered if they were one in the same?

"Cabin."

Flynn noticed the question in her voice. "Yes, just a one bedroom, but the couch has a pull out."

She smiled. "As long as it has an indoor bathroom and a stove, we're good."

He laughed at that. "Okay, lets check it out."

"Well, it is indoors," said Flynn, as they opened the door of the small bathroom.

"True, but from what century?"

"Probably the 1930s, I would guess." Flynn tried the sink tap in the kitchen and was satisfied that it was working fine despite the wooden slat counter top that surrounded it. "This camp was started in the 1930s and it would seem this is one of the first original cabins—living history right here." He spread his arms out, meant to encompass the entire rustic cabin.

Meg laughed. "The perfect ambiance for working on genealogies." She pulled out her laptop from its case, deciding the best place to set up. There was only one small table in the combination kitchen-living room area. "When are you due to go to Peterborough?"

Flynn checked his watch. "For ten o'clock. I should make it okay if I leave soon." He looked around and then glanced in the bedroom where there were bunk beds hugging the wall; a double bottom and a twin above. "Gran packed us some sheets and pillows and some towels. I'll bring them in before I leave. I'll bring in the cooler too, if you don't mind unpacking the items Martha packed for us."

Meg was surprised he had been so organized. "Sure, go ahead, I'll take care of everything."

"Thanks, I should be back by four." After unpacking his car, and a kiss goodbye, he was gone.

While sorting out the sheet sets Meg wondered how Alice knew which sheets to pack. Maybe Flynn came here a lot or perhaps all the facilities had the same sized beds. She was curious as to what other features this lodge offered so decided, once things were unpacked, and the food put away she would take a look around. Perhaps they could rent a boat for the evening after supper.

There was a knock at the door. "Hi, I'm Trevor, Flynn's friend. You must be Meg." He stood with the screen door ajar and held out his hand which Meg shook in return. "I hope you like it here. My family has owned the property for five generations now."

"It's a very beautiful place, I can't wait to explore. I'm eager to try the fishing too."

"Come up to the office and I'll give you a map of the lake and possible fishing hot spots."

She could feel him gauging her, possibly wondering what her relationship was with Flynn, as she followed Trevor to the office. He was tall like Flynn, and could have been his brother they were so much alike. Same dark complexion, same body shape, same hazel eyes and a pleasant smile.

Once inside, he rummaged through some papers on his desk and finally found the stack he was looking for; photocopied maps of the lake with contour lines and spots highlighted where different species of fish might be found.

"I must say," he went on, "when Flynn called me and asked for the old log cabin, I did wonder why he didn't want to take the two-bedroom cottage I had available, but now I've met you, and see your appreciation for the outdoors, maybe that explains it." He handed her the map with a smile.

Meg resisted the urge to comment further and just confirmed that everything was fine with their accommodations. *Interesting, so, he planned this. Then let's hope the couch is comfortable.*

"Flynn mentioned that you two were old friends. How did you two meet?"

He laughed at that. "We had both volunteered for Habitat for Humanity in, I think 2018. We ended up in Alberta for a few weeks and just hit it off. We've kept in touch ever since. Flynn often stays with me when he's working out of Peterborough. We often go camping together." Then he laughed softly. "You know, my father said to us once when Flynn and I were fishing with him not far from here—he knew we were at the age of looking for the right one—he'd say, 'If you are interested in a girl, take her camping and see what she brings with her. If she brings a suitcase full of cosmetics and hair supplies as well as her clothes, she's not the one for you.' He would give us a knowing look and I wondered briefly if that is how he found my mother." He laughed at the thought, then he gave Meg an appraising look and a soft smile. "I hear you brought a laptop for work and fishing gear."

She accepted the map with thanks and a chuckle, at his last remark, then continued her exploration of the camp. Young children could be heard playing along the beach area, and she walked over to see a few wooden Adirondack chairs, brightly coloured, occupied by some of the mothers of the children. The beach was long and sandy and the remains of several sand castles lined the upper areas, their design indicating that the mothers had helped with their construction. New construction was now taking place closer to the water, where the younger children could easily fetch water or splash once the novelty of sand castles wore off.

Moving back through a wooded area Meg went to check out the boating situation. There was a sign just above the docks that suggested renting canoes or kayaks, giving their price by the day. She noticed that the docking area was well maintained, its boards heavy and firm, with little chance of breaking. An older boy stood at one end of the many boat slips and was casting into the open spaces between the docks. Closer to the shore another boy was hunting for minnows with a long-handled net.

Meg turned and followed the trail that led to the three older cabins, the furthest being theirs. She noticed that the other two didn't seem to be occupied, and again the idea of him planning this crossed her thoughts. She wondered if Flynn had been testing her, and smiled at what Trevor had told her.

She would see if they could rent a canoe once Flynn got back, but for now she had some work to do.

Before they had left for their mini working vacation, Meg had found the siblings of Walter and Emily Fernsby. Now she would look into the families of those brothers and sisters, and see if any of Alice's cousins had a connection with the Canadian families. It was close to noon before she had finished with the Fernsbys, Mulfords and Robsons, finding nothing that seemed for the moment to be a connection with William and Anne Carter.

With lunch in mind, she decided to take a break and have one of the ham sandwiches Martha had packed for them. Perhaps a walk over to the docking side with her rod and a couple of her favourite lures might be in order. She would try as the boy had and see if there were any fish near the docks that might be tempted by a perch- coloured lure.

As Meg approached the docking area, she noticed that many of the early-morning fishermen had arrived back. Most of the slips were filled now and several men were gathered on shore in front of the bait and tackle shop, checking out the leader board that was posted on the outside wall. Apparently, there was a contest of some sort for the largest fish caught. There were three categories listed on the board: pike, pickerel and bass. Some men seemed disappointed that their catch from the previous day no longer qualified for first place, while others were elated, hopeful that their large catch for the morning might remain in first position.

"Hi, are you here for the derby?" A young man—tall, blonde, and well-tanned having noticed her, rod and reel in hand—approached her.

Meg smiled. "No, I just thought I would try my luck with a few casts. Maybe catch supper."

"You should enter," he said. "I heard a story from one of the fisherman about a guy who came up here last year. He'd never been fishing before and ended up catching a six-pound, eight-ounce pike. Everyone thought he had won first prize for sure." He laughed to himself. "But he hadn't entered the derby."

Meg smiled at that. A friend of the young man she was talking to, saw her and came over. She noticed him eyeing her up and down, and took an immediate dislike to him.

"Get lost, Roger." Reluctantly, his friend took the hint and left to rejoin their buddies.

"Don't mind him," said her new acquaintance. "He can't resist a pretty girl. And I'm afraid he's not too subtle about it at times."

"I'll walk you down to the docking area." He turned once more to make sure Roger wasn't intending to follow them. They made their way down the path to the stony shore where two long docks projected out into the lake with several perpendicular shorter docks attached on either side allowing boats to tie up when not in use.

Coming along the shore was Trevor making his way to the boathouse at the far end of the docking area, that housed canoes and extra motors while also allowing a place to make repairs.

He waved at them both. "Are you on the leader board yet, Pete?"

"Not yet, but we're going out again tonight, so maybe I'll get a prize winner."

"Are you going to try your luck at fishing now, Meg?"

She laughed. "Not really. I just wanted to practice my casting for a while."

Trevor nodded at that. "We sell fishing licences here, if yours isn't up to date."

"Oh no, I totally forgot. Thanks, Trevor, I'll do it now."

"My wife Cindy is there. She'll get you sorted out." With that he continued on up the beach.

"I suppose we've been informally introduced now. Nice meeting you, Meg." Pete inclined his head in a small bow. "Maybe I'll see you again before you leave."

"Thank you, Pete. Good luck with the derby."

She turned, fishing gear in hand and headed for the office. The door was open with just the screen door covering the entrance, but she could see a young woman sitting behind the counter, focused on the computer screen before her.

Cindy glanced up, having heard the screen door open. "Hello, welcome to the lodge," she said, realizing Meg was a new guest.

"Hi. Trevor said I might get a fishing licence here."

"Of course. You're Meg, aren't you?" She reached into the counter drawer and pulled out a form with a pamphlet outlining the rules and regulations. "Flynn mentioned you when he called for accommodations." She gave Meg a warm smile and a tilt of her head. "He didn't do you justice." She glanced at the board to her side that held the keys to all their cottages. "I feel bad that Flynn stuck you in that old cabin when it wasn't necessary; we did have a two-bedroom cottage available, if you'd like to trade."

Meg gave Cindy a knowing look and smiled. "Thank you, but no ... it's actually fine and besides I think the pull-out bed will be very comfortable for Flynn."

Cindy picked up the humour in her voice and laughed. "Well, then, let's get you ready for fishing. Do you have an Outdoors Card?"

"No, I think the last time I bought a licence was almost six years ago."

Cindy passed her the pamphlet. "First you need an Outdoors Card, that's just under ten dollars, then you have some choices: an actual fishing licence for one or three years or just for one day. If you choose the one, or three-year licence you can choose between a conservation licence or a sport licence. A conservation licence has reduced catch limits." Meg followed along in the booklet.

"What about a one-day licence. I see I can forgo the Outdoors Card if I just get a licence for one day."

"We can do that."

They'd come up on a Friday and would be staying, she thought, until Sunday, and didn't know how much fishing they would do or when, then changed her mind. "Let's get the 1-year then, I think I might be fishing more than one day."

Meg filled out the appropriate documentation for the conservation licence, then paid the fees required.

"There, you're all set," said Cindy, handing Meg her temporary permits.

"Flynn said you were a genealogist, is that how you met Flynn."

Meg smiled, knowing Cindy too was curious about her relationship with Flynn. "Yes, his grandmother hired me to find out more about her ancestors." Then she added, "We have been working on it together and I'll continue here too while he's at work." As an after thought she said, "I'm just glad you have the internet. Can't do much research without that."

"Well, I hope you enjoy your stay here."

"Thanks, Cindy."

Deciding to abandon her casting for now, and having acquired the correct documentation, just in case she did have a chance to go fishing, Meg made her way back to their cabin. Flynn would be back in a few hours, giving her enough time to set up ready for supper and get some more work done.

"Ah, so there you are, Calli Fernsby." It was her, formally Caroline Simpson, on the 1939 register entry she had just found, living with her mother and father. Proof of this lay in her wedding information to Walter's brother John. The parents' names matched, as well as her age. So, it was Caroline who had sent the wedding picture to Harold Fernsby all those years later.

Now it was time to begin a search back to Emily and Anne's cousins and then their children, if they had married. She'd start with Emily's parents; George and Alice Robson. The census records for 1921 and 1911 gave an indication as to their ages and place of birth. The 1921 record also told how many years they had been married, although sometimes that information was fudged a bit to coincide with the eldest child's birth, so it wasn't always accurate. By the time Flynn was expected back Meg had found Emily's parents' siblings and was about to start looking for all marriages and deaths when she heard the sound of someone out on the small wooden porch that held the steps up to the door.

Then his voice, "Honey, I'm home."

She smiled, then went to the door to greet him. "Hi, you're back early, good." He looked tired and after a long drive starting at five, and then working, no wonder. "Why don't you have a lie down until supper time. The couch is all made up for you."

He yawned involuntarily. "I might just do that. It's been a long day."

"Here." Meg handed him a cool drink. "Martha made up a thermos of iced tea."

Flynn took the proffered glass and walked over to the couch. After giving her and the couch a dubious look, took off his shoes and sat down, bouncing a bit to check the firmness. "I should only need an hour," he said again, yawning, then placing his empty glass on the end table, fluffed his pillow and fell back onto the made-up bed.

Meg pulled the blanket she had found in the cupboard, up over him then quietly took up her place at the table and worked as he slept. Occasionally she would glance over at him and watch him sleep, his face relaxed and softened in sleep made him look much younger than he was, which made her smile.

She had finished finding George Robson's brothers; James and Edward. George's wife Alice Shipley, had three brothers and one sister: Albert, William, Joseph and Emily. Emily Fernsby must have been named after this aunt. She was just about to start looking into possible marriages, when Flynn stirred.

He sat up, yawned and rubbed his face. He looked around and saw her working on her computer. "I needed that nap. Thanks."

"I'm glad. I saw a sign that showed canoes for rent. Maybe after supper we can rent one and do some fishing."

"I'd like that too," said Flynn. He checked his watch. "I'll go and arrange it before the office closes." She could hear him splashing water on his face in the bathroom.

Upon emerging, he looked around at the small area that passed for a kitchen; a four-foot wooden prep-counter with sink and a two-door cupboard above and a two-door cabinet below with one door off its hinge. "What did Martha send for supper? I'm starving, I didn't get a lunch break."

Meg laughed. "Burgers, potato salad, tomatoes, and wine."

Flynn chuckled at the list. "She does know me, doesn't she." He stood on the small deck before leaving. "I'll start the barbecue first."

Chapter 14

The water was like glass, and their canoe glided smoothly along the shore of a small island in the middle of the lake. "I can't think of a more perfect evening," said Meg. She dipped her paddle in and watched as it created small wavelets. The sun was low in the sky but would provide light for another hour. They had been paddling for quite a while, as Flynn was eager to show her some of his favourite spots. Meg had her fishing rod with her and two of her favourite lures.

"What about here?" she asked.

"This is a good spot. If we go between the island and the shore."

Meg placed her paddle back in the boat behind her.

"I can paddle if you want to troll, or do you want to just cast out for a while?"

Meg considered the two options and having seen how fast the canoe moved through the water, chose trolling. She turned so she could face Flynn and let the line out slowly after Flynn nodded in agreement.

It had been a few years since she had been fishing, but had never considered getting rid of her fishing equipment. She'd kept fishing alive in honour of her father. He had loved the sport and would often stop the family car near any small pond or creek and pull his rod from the trunk, and test the waters for fish. Meg would leave the car too, abandoning her mother to sit patiently while Meg stood beside her father, watching, learning as he cast with his favourite lure. He rarely caught anything, but that didn't matter, it was the time they spent together she treasured.

"Oh, something touched the lure."

"Maybe weeds," suggested Flynn.

"Maybe. Oh! Got it." The line pulled and her rod bent. "I don't think it's big but it's very strong."

Flynn kept paddling as Meg played the fish and reeled it in slowly. It didn't take long, and he heard the fish hit the side of the boat as she hauled her catch in. He smiled at the look on her face. She smiled. "A Pumpkinseed, I haven't seen one of those in years." The fish, the shape of large Sunfish but without the sunny coloured yellow bottom, had a large black pumpkin seed-like spot next to its gills.

"It's a big one too. Shall I take it off for you?"

The fish hung conveniently dangling in front of Flynn's face. "Thank you, yes."

"He's just hooked in the lip." Flynn unhooked the lure, and with a nod from Meg released it back into the water. "Do you want to try again?"

The sun was beginning to set, and it would take a good half hour to get back to the camp. "Why don't we paddle back before it gets dark and maybe have our fire." Flynn had purchased two milk crates of fire wood before they had left on their ride.

"I'd like that, and I'm getting hungry too."

The kindling had caught easily, once the paper below it flamed. The larger logs, of maple burned well now and flames rose up like coloured fingers of gold. The odd crackle from the wood as it settled, sent up sparks that flew up like fireflies in the dark. "This is nice. I don't often sit out and watch the stars," said Meg. She sat back in the wooden chair and looked up into the sky. "Look! A shooting star!" She pointed up as the star disappeared into the blackness.

Flynn looked to where she pointed. "It's different from the city isn't it. No city lights to compete with." He looked at the fire they had made in a pit behind their cabin, and added another log causing a few sparks to explode upward, burning out before landing on the ground. "How do you like your hotdog?" He raised up the stick he had found, carved into a point that now held a slightly blackened wiener.

Meg laughed. "I think that one will do fine." She leaned over with a bun in hand and grabbed the wiener, sliding it from the stick.

Flynn put on another wiener for himself and poured a glass of wine for Meg, then himself. "I should be back earlier tomorrow. That should give me some time to work with you on the cousins."

Meg swallowed her first bite of the hotdog with a "Hmmmmm" of satisfaction, before answering. "I think I would like you to work on that newspaper picture. It might give us some names that hopefully have a connection with the names we have so far, or may come up later."

"I should be back by two tomorrow, so I can start then." He removed the stick from the fire and slid the wiener off of its wooden skewer, with the toasted bun he had.

"I rented the canoe for the time we're here so if you like you can use it tomorrow before I get back." He took a bite of his meal and sighed.

"Thanks, I might do that."

Then a thought occurred to Flynn. "What do we tell Gran if we can't find a connection?"

Meg swallowed then shook her head slightly. She'd been wondering the same thing but didn't want to admit defeat. "We'll find it. I know we will."

A charred log fell in the fire, burnt through, and caused sparks that floated upward. "Shall I put another log on?"

"It's getting late, maybe we should call it a night. You have to go to work tomorrow."

Flynn reached across and took her hand in his. "True, it's been a beautiful night. And I'm looking forward to a good night's sleep."

Flynn rolled over, the comforter only half covering him. It seemed to be early morning. He opened the one eye that wasn't pressed against the pillow and saw Meg at the small stove cooking.

Bacon. The smell moved him so both eyes were focused on the scene before him. Meg looked his way.

"One egg or two?" she asked.

He smiled. "Two please. Do we have a toaster?"

"Yes, so toast too?"

He nodded, still half asleep. "What time is it?"

"Just after seven. Get yourself ready. You have fifteen minutes before breakfast is ready." He swung his legs off the bed and sat, trying hard to wake up.

"Did you sleep well?" He noticed the slight curve of her lips as she asked.

"Yes. Quite well actually," he amended, trying not to let her see the stretching he did to alleviate the kink in his back.

The pull-out couch had been comfortable, as far as a thin mattress on a thin layer of springs could be comfortable. Between the bed and his brain not winding down from thinking, he had just about five hours sleep.

He had kissed Meg goodnight and given her a warm embrace, then she had said, "goodnight" and gently closed the bedroom door, not giving his sleeping accommodations a second thought. He bit his lip. He could have been sleeping in a nice bed in one of Trevor's nice cottages. Oh well, he had chosen this rough cabin for a reason so he couldn't complain when Meg didn't offer to share the bedroom with him, even if there was a bed that wasn't being used.

He rubbed his hands across his face trying to wake up. He had just a few minutes to get himself ready. It was Saturday, and once he'd finished helping Sherman at the office, he was free for the rest of the weekend.

It was a hot day. The sun streamed in through the small window by the kitchen, but also brought with it a slight breeze that flowed through the cabin and out through the door which she had left open, leaving the screen door to prevent bugs from coming in. Flynn had left for work leaving her to clean up after breakfast, and tidy the sleeping areas. She had smiled as she straightened up the bed coverings on the pull-out bed before she pushed it back under, making it into a couch once more.

It was eleven o'clock now and she sat in front of her computer hunting for the cousins of Emily Fernsby. Emily's maiden name was Robson, and Meg had found her family on the 1921 census. Her parents were George Robson and Alice Shipley. It gave her heart a small squeeze when she saw that Flynn's grandmother was named after her own grandmother. As she had discovered already, Alice Shipley had four siblings: Emily, Albert, William and Joseph. George had two brothers: Edward and James. Now she would check for marriages.

"Hello." Someone was on the small porch, calling into the cabin through the screen door.

"Yes?" Meg left her work and went to see who was at the door. Perhaps it was Trevor wanting to speak with Flynn.

"Oh, morning, Pete."

Pete stood, holding a net with a very large fish. "You are looking at the number three fish now on the leader board." He stood smiling, proud of his early morning catch, a thin trail of water or fish slime, Meg couldn't tell which, streaming from the net.

"That's wonderful."

Pete beamed his pleasure. "Would you care to have a fish lunch with me?" he asked.

"Thank you, I'd like that. I need a break."

He looked around the front area of the cabin. "Is there a fire pit for this cabin?" he asked.

"Yes, around the back."

"Good, I'll be back in twenty minutes.

That gave Meg time to find some dishes. She opened up both cupboard doors and found plates and mugs that she could use. She pulled out the drawer at the bottom of the stove and found a large cast iron frying pan that would do well to fry fish over a fire.

It didn't take that long, and Pete was back with the fish fillets wrapped in some newspaper, and a small box with a bottle of cooking oil, a small onion and three potatoes, an egg, a small bag of what looked like flour and a box of breadcrumbs.

"Wow, you did come prepared." Meg was rewarded with a smile.

Pete glanced at the remainder of the firewood that Flynn had purchased. There was just enough for another fire. "Why don't I get the fire going, if you don't mind fixing the potatoes and breading the fish."

"I can do that, and I'll meet you outside." Then she added, "I found a large cast iron pan too, we can use for frying."

"Perfect," said Pete, as he removed the cooking oil from the box then handed the remaining ingredients to Meg.

Meg took the proffered box and went back inside allowing the screen door to slam behind her. She peeled and cut the potatoes in thin strips, then sliced the onion, which she assumed Pete would add to the oil for flavour. She'd had fish fries before and knew that some people prepared their fish differently, but the flour, egg and bread crumbs told her that Pete fixed his fish the same way she usually did. She unwrapped the meaty fillets of fish, and cut them in smaller chunks, to make them easier to bread. When she was finished, she took a bowl of potatoes and a tray of breaded fish and onions outside.

Pete had a decent fire made by this time and smiled when he saw her bring out the tray. "Perfect," he said. He placed the tray on a cut log that acted as a small table someone had set by the fire pit. Pete hadn't brought any cooking utensils, reasoning that all the cottages had similar tools for lifting and straining.

Meg went back inside to get the dishes and utensils they would need. The smell of onions cooking in the hot oil suddenly gave Meg an appetite. She loved the smell of food cooking over an open fire.

"Oh, my. This is so good." Meg noticed that Pete was pleased that she was enjoying the fish. "Thank you for inviting me." She took another cautious bite of her second piece of fish, as Pete had warned her to be careful, in case he had missed a few bones.

"I'm glad you're enjoying it," he said, as he finished up his fries. He looked at her questioning. "What do you do for a living?"

"I'm a genealogist," Meg said, after taking a small drink from her tumbler. "I help people discover their family roots." He seemed to find that very interesting, and she smiled. "We're working on a family now, that has connections in England."

"Do you find many clients? I mean I wouldn't think there would be that many people that would pay to find out about their ancestors."

Meg laughed at that. "You'd be surprised ..."

"Hi," said a familiar voice. Having smelled the fire smoke, Flynn walked around the cabin to find Meg and Pete sitting by a fire that had almost burned itself out.

"Come join us," said Meg. "Pete invited me to share in his version of a shore lunch."

Pete stood up to greet him. "Glad to meet you, I'm Flynn, Meg's ... associate."

"Pete Dawson," said Pete. He smiled, but Meg could see the thought cross his face wondering what her relationship with Flynn was.

Meg moved over and made room for Flynn next to her. "Have you had lunch? There's more fish."

166

Flynn looked to Pete for confirmation. "Don't let it go to waste," agreed Pete and he held out the platter that contained the few remaining pieces.

"Thanks, I left the office earlier than I expected." He bit into the still warm fish. "This is good, is it pickerel?"

"Yes, and it might just be a prize winner. It wasn't at the maximum slot size but very wide and heavy, so we will see by Sunday if I go home with the third prize." He laughed. "For now, my name is at least on the leader board."

Meg watched as the two men exchanged pleasantries, and wondered what Flynn must be thinking. But then what did it matter, they weren't an exclusive couple yet and she was only having lunch, yet something made her feel a bit guilty; that she should explain, not that she would. There was nothing to explain. A fisherman had asked her to lunch and that was all there was to it.

The two were now exchanging fishing stories and discussing types of lures and Meg laughed to herself. Her worries about an explanation vanished and she finished her last piece of fish listening as Flynn gave Pete some advice.

"You go past Colonel Island and find camping spot forty-two on the left, then just to the right of the sandy beach there is a large weed bed. It's shallow and you'll find lots of bass there, especially around seven-thirty. You might even take the lead in the bass category if you get a big one there."

"Thanks, I'll try it tonight. This is my first year here and I'm just learning where the good spots are." Pete stood and bowed formally to Meg. "Thank you for sharing lunch with me, Meg."

"I enjoyed the fish very much. Thank you for asking me." Meg glanced briefly at Flynn who was enjoying the last piece of fish. "I'll get your box for you," she said and left the two men alone.

When she came back with the remains of the ingredients Pete had brought, Flynn was telling Pete of another good spot for bass. Meg shook her head. She wasn't really sure Flynn would be jealous or not but the fact that he wasn't somehow annoyed her. And admitting that, annoyed her more.

"Thanks, Meg," said Pete, taking the box he had brought with the remnants left. "Thanks for the tips, Flynn. You'll know if they worked if you see my name on the board tomorrow."

Meg and Flynn both watched as Pete walked back towards the cottages.

"I like Pete," said Flynn turning, and gave her a smile. Then he addressed the cast iron pan that sat cooling on the log table. "I'll dump the oil in the fire pit once it cools down."

He reached out to take Meg's hand then drew her close. He embraced her in a warm hug then stepped back to gave her a solid kiss. "Now that we've had lunch, I'm ready to look for that newspaper picture."

Chapter 15

They sat in silence, each working on different sites; Flynn searching newspapers and Meg working on finding more about Emily's cousins.

After another fifteen minutes, Flynn exploded in triumph. "I found the picture!"

He turned his screen so Meg could see the happy couple. Meg gave his arm a quick squeeze in congratulations.

"It's a bit sharper too, and they actually have the names of those in the picture." Flynn was excited and so pleased he had found it.

"Take a screen shot of the page," said Meg, "and then we can print a copy of the paper itself when we get back." She zoomed in and read the names under the picture.

"Walter Fernsby and his bride Emily Fernsby formally Robson. Bride's maids, Sarah Cotter, Bettes Newman, Lorraine Weatherby and Wendy Collier." None of the names matched any they had discovered so far on the Canadian side.

"Where are you with the cousins?"

Meg checked her notes. "I have all the siblings of George and Alice Robson. I just have to check now for their marriages and possible children."

"Where can I help?" said Flynn, suddenly feeling confident that they would be successful after finding the wedding picture.

"Here, you can work on George Robson's siblings." Meg passed him a list of the George's brothers. "I'll carry on with his wife's four siblings. Here, use this site."

Flynn copied the address and proceeded to the genealogy site he had used once before back at his grandmothers."

They worked quietly until Flynn broke the silence by asking, "Did you enjoy your lunch with Pete?"

Meg smiled to herself but tried to keep her face impassive. "Yes, he seems nice. We met yesterday down by the dock area."

There was silence from Flynn for a moment then an, "Oh," followed.

"I hope he wins the derby," she added.

"Yeah, me too," he said, almost to himself. Meg smiled, happy now.

It was another ten minutes before Meg said, "Found something."

Flynn leaned over to view her screen. "Alice Robson's sister Emily Shipley married a William Newman. They had four children; Dorothy, Elizabeth, and Alice, and a brother Frederick. Isn't Bettes a shortened form of Elizabeth."

"I think so, yes," said Flynn following on the chart Meg had drawn on her writing pad. "So, you found Emily Fernsby's cousin from the wedding photo."

"It seems so, yes. I just have to check now and see if any of the siblings married and had any children."

"How are you making out with George Robson's brothers?"

"Nothing here, they both died in WW1 and left no family behind."

Meg checked her list. "Could you check out Albert, William and Joseph, while I work on the Newmans."

"Sure."

It was starting to get late and they had been working almost three hours and it was getting close to supper time. Meg realized that Flynn had had just two small pieces of fish for lunch and thought maybe they should eat earlier today. "Why don't I start to get supper ready, while you work. You must be getting hungry."

"Actually, I am. What did Martha send that we could have?"

"Burgers?"

"Great." He sat back from the computer. "I need to get some more wood first, then I'll get the fire going again and we can cook them on the grill."

Meg could easily cook the patties on the stove but like Flynn agreed that burgers tasted better cooked over a flame. Meg could tell he was tired, and readily agreed. They could look up records later.

"I'll get the rest ready, then."

Flynn got up, stretched, a bit stiff after sitting, and left to go and start the fire up again.

❧

"I'm sorry ..." He leaned back, looking up at the shimmering leaves of the tree overhead. "If I acted a bit..." He glanced at Meg to see if she had any inkling as to what he was talking about.

Meg smiled, then took his hand in hers and squeezed it in reassurance. "That's okay, I'm sure Pete didn't take any notice." Then she switched the topic. "It was nice of you to give him some good spots to fish. I wonder if he came back with any winning fish tonight?"

He gave her hand a squeeze back then took up the stick he was using as a poker and gave the fire a bit of a poke. It was late; the moon had risen and cast its light through the leaves of the trees. The clouds, few as they were, pausing only briefly as they passed like ghosts across its face.

"I was wondering ..." Meg began, "how uncomfortable your couch might be?"

Flynn gave her a knowing look and a smile crossed his face. "It's not so bad. I've slept on worse."

"Well, I thought," she said, feeling guilty now, "there's an extra bed made up. It's small, but it might be better than the couch."

He stood and pulled her up close to him, then leaned in for a kiss that was solid, soft and lingering. He leaned back and smiled. "It's only one more night. Come on."

Flynn covered the fire first, then they walked back to the cabin.

"Well, I've found all of the Newman children, all I need to do now is check out their marriages and any possible children," said Meg. "But first I'll check the 1939 directory and see which spouse names I'm looking for."

"I finished with Albert, William and Joseph. All three joined the army in 1914. Albert came home after being gassed in France. He died ten years later. William and Joseph both died at the battle of the Somme. There was a write-up in the paper about them." He leaned over to see the list she had. "Which ones do you want me check?"

"Here, you can look into Alice and Frederick Newman and I'll continue with Dorothy, Elizabeth and William."

There was a tentative knock at the door and a man with the sun behind him, cast a shadow across the screen. "Come on in," called Flynn, who had risen now to greet the visitor.

Pete was all smiles. "They are going to announce the winners soon. I thought, if you weren't busy, you'd like to see how I made out."

"Sure," said Meg, joining them. "We need a break anyway."

Flynn nodded in agreement and the three made their way back to the docking side of the lodge where a large crowd of fishermen and their supporters were standing, amid wooden Adirondack chairs, small cedar trees and picnic tables, waiting for Trevor to emerge from the office and join them.

Finally, Trevor came out with his wife Cindy who was holding several envelopes, probably the money prize for first prize in each category, Meg thought. They had the leaderboard up on a small table leaning against a tree with the final results. Prizes for second and third were laid out on a longer table. Everyone waited for Trevor to speak.

"We had a great derby this year. We had eighty-seven entrants and as of ten o'clock this morning, we have our winners. In the pickerel category- first prize goes to Pete Dawson for a two pound-five-ounce pickerel." Everyone clapped as Pete went up to receive his winning envelope. The clapping continued as second and third prizes were accepted by the pickerel winners. Pete walked back and stood next to Meg and Flynn and joined in congratulating the other winners.

"Now for the bass category. First prize goes to Pete Dawson for a four pound-six- ounce bass."

Again, the clapping began as Pete went forward to receive his prize envelope. Flynn gave him a warm clap on the shoulder. "Good job!"

When the second and third prizes were announced, Pete gave Flynn a big smile and went to acknowledge his second prize for bass; a pizza oven and portable bar-be-cue.

All three waited politely for the remaining prizes to be distributed.

"That spot by forty-two brought in the winners," said Pete, again thanking Flynn for his fishing advice.

"I'm glad," said Flynn. "Maybe next year I will enter and give you a run for the money."

Pete said his farewells, then went to pick up his prize that sat at one end of the prize table.

Meg and Flynn walked back hand in hand past the office and through the wooded area back to their cabin.

People who had come to the lodge specifically for the derby could be heard heading home now that the prizes had been awarded. You could hear the odd slam of a screen door as men loaded up their trucks, or a car following the road out of camp.

It would be a lot quieter now too, with most of the camp vacant, that is until the start of the next week brought in a new group of vacationers.

Flynn's job was done and he decided to stay a bit longer and leave the next morning. Meg had agreed and they would work a few more hours before calling it quits for the day and take some time to enjoy the surroundings.

Meg reminded him that they didn't need to go past the 1939 registry as anything from 1940 going forward would be useless because Alice was already living in Canada.

"I found out who Lorraine Weatherby was," said Flynn, turning his screen towards Meg so she could see the marriage record; Lorraine Weatherby had married Frederick Newman in 1932, in London.

"Emily's cousin's wife. Good, so we add another name that might link to Anne Carter." She smiled. "Somehow I think we are on the right trail."

Meg enlarged the page she was looking at and gave a small sound of triumph. "I just found William Newman on the '39 and his wife, Bettes. So, it wasn't his sister who was mentioned in the wedding picture, it was William's wife. Now all I need to do is check out their marriage and find out what her maiden name was."

Ten minutes later Flynn heard an exclamation from Meg. She had the look of a gold miner who had just discovered a wall of gold in a hidden cave.

He leaned over to see. Meg was smiling from ear to ear and just pointed to her find.

"You did it. Oh my …"

Meg had found the marriage of William Newman to Elizabeth Ramsey; Anne Carter's globe trotting sister.

"Do you think they were the ones who brought Alice to Canada."

"I think it's quite possible and there's only one way to find out. We search passenger lists and see if they came over between 1938 and 1939."

"I'm almost afraid to look," said Flynn "just in case we don't find it."

Meg leaned back in her chair, her eyes, tired. "Why don't we leave it then until we're back at you grandmother's place. It's almost lunch time and we can go for a walk through the woods or something."

"I agree. Gran might like to be there when we do prove our theory."

"Can you eat them?"

Meg looked closer at the polypore fungus that had grown on the remains of a dead birch tree branch. "I've heard they are rather bitter tasting. I do know that people used to or maybe still do in a pinch, used the underside strips as a band-aid for cuts because it is antibacterial and stops wounds from bleeding. I think it is used for medicine too but I'm not sure how."

She looked around. "Now, there's one you can eat." She pointed out a white mushroom with bright bubble gum gills, growing in a grassy space between two large trees. "It's called a meadow mushroom. I know most of the edible ones." Then she laughed. "But I usually eat the ones I find in the market."

Flynn kneeled down to get a better look. "That's probably a wise choice, although if you were lost in the woods, I don't suppose you'd go hungry."

"I think I'd be okay."

They walked quite a ways inland then turned back towards the lake and walked along the rugged shore looking for colourful stones or sand-washed bits of coloured glass.

The land on the far side of them jutted out into the water and they could hear a few branches breaking. They stood still looking. "I've only seen one here once before. This one looks larger," said Flynn in a whisper.

A moose, having come to the water's edge for a drink, suddenly looked up in their direction. "We're down wind from him so if we are quiet, he may not be frightened off."

They stood watching for several minutes, until the large animal wandered back into the bush. "He was beautiful," said Meg.

Just before they reached the docking area, Flynn stopped and took Meg's hand, pulling her gently to him. 'Have I told you, lately, how beautiful you are?"

She smiled. "Yes." She leaned in for a kiss. His arms engulfed her and she suddenly felt safe and cared for.

"Come on, you must be getting hungry." They walked back towards their cabin.

"How do steaks sound tonight?"

"Sounds perfect."

Chapter 16

"Here, try this one," said Flynn, reaching over and handing her the new lure.

"A jitterbug! Where did you find it?"

"I knew you didn't have any bass lures with you, so I looked in the tack shop and found this."

The jitterbug, had a black, torpedo-shaped body like a large bug, and a spooned piece of metal attached horizontally to the front of the lure, that when cast made a 'glub-glub' sound as it was reeled slowly back in. Meant for night bass fishing, it was the perfect time to try it. Bass were attracted by sound at night so as long as a lure made a noise it would attract them.

They'd gone past camp site forty-two as Flynn had described to Pete and had found the large weed bed.

Flynn back paddled so they were on the edge of the weeds so Meg could cast out without the danger of getting snagged.

He sat still and watched with admiration as Meg gave her rod a flick of the wrist and the lure sailed out into the darkness. It was a full moon with little cloud and although Flynn had considered the wisdom of paddling out so far from the lodge, he was confident they could return without incident.

Meg smiled as the noisy lure designed to attract bass, made its way back to her, the glub-glub sound hopefully attracting attention, whether it was from hunger or annoyance at the sound she wasn't sure.

"Got one!"

The splash beyond their vision indicated a large fish. Meg reeled in slowly, her rod bending, but keeping the line still taut. The fish jumped again with the forlorn hope of dislodging the lure.

Meg took her time hoping to tire out her catch before bringing it closer to the canoe.

"Here, come more towards me." Not having a net, Flynn reached out and took the line as Meg reeled in the slack, then together they lifted the fish into the bottom of their canoe.

"It's a nice bass," said Flynn as he reached down and took the fish by its lip and unhooked the lure. "He's lucky; he's only caught in the upper lip." He held up the fish for Meg to see its actual size.

Meg smiled, watching how Flynn handled the animal. She had always been taught to show respect for living things and was glad they shared that.

"It's your lucky day fish. We've already had supper; so back you go."

"You heard what she said," Flynn said, facing the fish as if directly talking to it, then gently released it back into the dark water. It gave a sudden splash and disappeared into the night.

Meg looked up at the moon. Its light had made a shimmering trail on the water. "It's gotten a lot darker, should we head back?"

It would take a good half hour to get back, and that was with both of them paddling. Flynn nodded, and waited for Meg to pick up her paddle and turn around. There was little wind but they stayed close to shore on their way. Without lights it was too risky to cut across any wide expanse of water in case they couldn't be seen by other boats heading back to the lodge.

The dipping of the paddles, suddenly brought to mind a poem she had learned in grade school, entitled- *The Song My Paddle Sings*. She listened as her paddle slid into the water and pushed back then lifted and slid into the water again. They paddled in unison, the time going by as they each enjoyed the night's silence. She could feel the dampness of the night begin to settle on them and the canoe. She couldn't remember having a better time.

Thank goodness for the dock floodlights that guided them back like a beacon in the night. Tired and weak from kneeling and paddling they pulled the canoe up onto the beach, next to the other canoes that lay overturned, waiting, ready for anyone who wanted to rent one for the day.

Camp fires dotted the grounds as cottagers enjoyed the evening outside. There were shouts from a few children, still at the camp, as they played hide 'n seek among the ghostly trees. Meg could smell hotdogs roasting over the open flames which brought back memories of her and her family doing similar activities over burning logs.

There was a call from one of the groups who were enjoying the evening outside.

"Come and join us," said Trevor. "We've got lots if you're hungry."

Flynn looked to Meg, who nodded. "I wouldn't mind something to eat right now," she admitted.

They joined the group of four, setting their rods against the building. Trevor and Cindy lived at the back-half of the office building and tonight were enjoying a fire with some of their guests.

Some of the fishermen had stayed on after the derby and Meg was pleased to see Pete—minus Roger—seated at the fire with Trevor and his wife Cindy. An older gentleman named Norm introduced himself as Pete slid over and made room for Meg to sit beside him on a wide bench that was close enough to the fire to feel its heat.

Flynn sat next to Cindy on the bench opposite them across from the fire and smiled to himself as he saw how Pete eagerly engaged in conversation with Meg.

Cindy handed Flynn a hotdog bun and he slid a roasted wiener off the metal skewer she used for cooking over a fire. Pete followed her example and handed his to Meg. "Ketchup or mustard?" he asked.

"This is fine, just the way it is," she said, and took a big bite of the proffered hotdog. She laughed after swallowing. "I wasn't a bit hungry until I smelled the cooking then all of a sudden I was starving. This is so good."

Flynn covered his dog with mustard and followed her example, like her, suddenly appreciating the roasted food.

"You're out a bit late tonight," said Trevor. "Bass fishing?"

"Yes. Meg caught a nice bass."

"It was the lure," said Meg. "Bass can't resist a jitterbug. We had a nice time paddling too. The lake is so peaceful and calm at night."

"True." said Trevor. "There aren't many boats on the lake at night."

"You should enter the derby next year," suggested Pete, addressing Meg before taking a bite of his own hotdog.

"We might just do that," replied Flynn, before Meg could respond.

Meg noticed Cindy turn and give Trevor one of those marital looks and smiled to herself.

It was well after twelve, when they started back towards their cabin. A loon on the lake gave a ghostly call, and another further away answered. Meg stood still and listened. Most of the other cottagers had retired earlier and the night was dark and quiet. "I've had a wonderful time," said Meg. "Thank you for suggesting I come along."

"I'm glad you're here too," admitted Flynn. He reached out and put his arm around her waist, then drew her closer. Her long hair had been clipped back and he reached around with his free hand and unclipped it, letting it fall around her shoulders.

His hand cupped her head as he leaned in for a kiss. Meg reached around his shoulders in an embrace and returned the affection, as they stood, for several moments, the loon calling again into the night.

Alice was waiting for them as they pulled into her driveway, having been alerted by Flynn that they were only a few minutes away.

She saw the look on their faces as they approached her, grinning like the Cheshire Cat. They either had a very good time together or they had found something exciting in the research. As much as she hoped they had enjoyed each other she also hoped they had found something new about her parents.

"Welcome back."

Meg ran over from the car and gave her a big hug. "We had a wonderful time, and ..." She glanced at Flynn, who nodded giving her the permission to share their find. "You'll never guess. We found the connection between Anne Carter and Emily Fernsby."

The look on Alice's face was worth the search, and when they found her in the passenger lists it would be wonderful.

"Come and have some lunch," Alice said. "Martha's made some wonderful quiche."

It felt good to get back in the library, where they had started this search.

"I feel so positive today. I needed those few days to get focused again."

"I enjoyed my days at the lodge too," said Meg. She gave Flynn a knowing look, and much to his credit he had the good grace to give her a sheepish look in return. "We need to figure this out, today." He nodded in agreement.

She opened up the site they had used for the past few weeks and Flynn did the same with the site he was use to using.

"Okay, start by looking for William Newman coming to Canada in 1939, plus or minus 2 years."

It didn't take long. Meg was the first to exclaim her find, "William Newman with wife Elizabeth. They had four children with them: William, George, Geoffrey and ..." She waved her fists in triumph. "Alice! Your grandmother."

"You know, I must have seen this before when I was searching for the name Alice in the passenger lists, and just thought as the list included other children she was also theirs. Oh, Flynn, I'm so excited, and so happy for Alice." Then her face fell, considering. It meant too that the parents she had known all her life were not her parents at all. Her people were in England.

Flynn leaned over and read the passenger list again. "Oh, Meg. She will be so happy that we have figured it out. But true there is the down side to this too." He looked at her and took her hand in his. "Now I'm not so sure we should have started this search."

He sat back and sighed. "I'm wondering now if this was a mistake. Should she know the truth?"

Meg stared at the screen contemplating Flynn's words. "Yes, now that we have spoken to Harold, we need to tell her, for her sake as well as his." There was another person to consider too. Someone who had never lost hope in finding his sister. "We owe it to them as well."

Flynn nodded. It was true.

They met Alice in the garden, just before supper. She sat watching the tiny birds hunt for the bread scraps she had thrown down for them. She smiled warmly at them as they entered through the new doors that now led from the library.

Flynn went to sit by her. She looked at him and for a moment he thought perhaps she knew the truth all along. "We have some news,' he said and he took her hand in his.

"We finally figured out the truth of how Harold claims to be your brother." She looked hopefully a him and smiled.

"It's alright, Flynn. You can tell me. I think perhaps I already know, but it would be good to hear what you have found that will prove it."

Meg took up the explanation from here. "Your mother Anne Carter had a sister Elizabeth. She went to England at some point, and we don't know how they met, but she married Emily Fernsby's cousin William Newman. Apparently Emily and her were very close. Elizabeth was at Walter and Emily's wedding in 1933. In 1939 they came to Canada with their three sons and you. We initially missed it because the ship's passenger list had her down as one of their children."

Alice studied the printout of the passenger list that Meg handed her.

Alice looked from Meg to Flynn and then a small smile lightened her face.

"So, I suppose we should let Harold know what you have found. I'm sure he will be very happy."

Flynn looked at Meg, glad that his grandmother had accepted their find without question. She looked pleased to have found her family but Flynn wondered if she also had regrets in starting this whole process.

"I'll send an email to Alicia and arrange a call for tomorrow," said Flynn.

Alice nodded. "I'd like to talk to him."

1946 Toronto, Ontario, Canada

It was a short telegram, delivered by the same boy who had delivered the news about William's captivity. This time he was smiling, having realized that her husband made it through the war. Anne waited until he had left before opening it. Alice had come to the door with her and now peered at the telegram.

"Is it from Daddy?" she asked.

Anne opened up the telegram.

MY DEAREST STOP I ARRIVE IN TORONTO BY TRAIN JANUARY 15 TWO O'CLOCK STOP I CAN'T WAIT TO SEE YOU AGAIN STOP LOVE STEVEN

"Yes, dear. It's from Daddy, he's coming home." She turned wiping away a tear then gave her daughter a hug. Hurry and get your coat Alice, we have to get to the train station.

2022 Niagara, Ontario, Canada

Alice sat in front of the computer screen, hesitant, both eager to share their news and also wondering how this news would affect Harold. She was aware of his fragile condition and hoped she wouldn't be making it worse by speaking to him.

The computer made its low beeping sound, waiting for a response from the other party being called.

"Hallo," said Alicia. The screen was still blank as Alicia found the button that allowed video. Harold, like Alice, sat in front of the screen, his face mirroring Alice's in Canada.

Alice spoke first, "Hello, brother."

"Brother?"

"Yes, we have discovered the link between your parents and my ... adopted parents."

Alicia moved next to her father so she was in the picture as well. The smile on her face contagious and Flynn and Meg sat behind Alice with the exact same expression.

"That's so wonderful," said Harold, as tears slowly left his eyes and slid down his cheeks.

"Yes, your mother's cousin William married my ... mother's sister Elizabeth. It was they who brought me to Canada for safe keeping in 1939."

Alicia gave her father a hug. "I'm so glad Auntie, this means the world to my father."

The call was short, enabling Harold to consider their news in private. They would resume with a longer call again tomorrow.

After the call Flynn ran back to the kitchen to get the bottle of champagne he had bought the day before and four glasses. He took Martha's hand and invited her to join them, she was after all considered part of Alice's family.

Alice looked at the chart that hung up on the library wall; her family just a few weeks ago, as Flynn entered the room. She had been so proud of their findings.

Meg stood beside her looking at all the names they had found for William and Anne Carter; the French bride of 1668, the Mohawk marriage, and all the names that stemmed from those.

"I suppose I won't be applying for membership in the Society of the Daughters of the King, any time soon," Alice said, laughing.

"Although," she started, smiling. "Some of these people are still part of my family, in a way; through my mother's cousin's wife."

Flynn passed the glasses around, filling each with their celebratory champagne. Martha stood by Alice; their free hands linked. "To family," he said, raising his glass. Meg, Martha and Alice did likewise and clinked them in a toast.

Flynn fished out an envelope from his jacket pocket and handed it to Meg.

"What is this?" she asked.

Flynn smiled, eager for her to find out. The envelope wasn't sealed and he watched as she withdrew the contents.

"Tickets?"

"Yes, for the three of us, to London." He gave his grandmother a hug, she smiled too, obviously in on the surprise.

Then it dawned on her, Harold lived in London. "Two weeks. To visit your brother," she said finally, excited for Alice. "Flynn, how nice."

"There's more."

Meg removed the paper that had been folded up behind the tickets and read the confirmation for a ten-day reservation he had made. "A castle? In Scotland?"

Flynn laughed at her bewilderment. "Can you think of a better place for a honeymoon? That is if you'll have me."

Before Meg could comment, Flynn had knelt down and was holding a ring in his hand. "Meg Fletcher, I love you. Will you marry me?"

She gave a questioning look at Alice, who smiled, as he placed the ring on her finger.

"I suppose I'll have to, now; you've bought the tickets." She laughed softly then added, "I love you too and of course, I'll marry you."

About the Author

Jacqueline Opresnik lives in Ontario, Canada, with her husband Frank and Bengal cat Tiggy. She received her degree in mathematics and geology from Brock University. She earned her pilot's licence shortly after, where she met her husband. Jackie pursued a teaching career and taught in the elementary grades. She has had a love of writing since she was ten and is just now beginning to fulfill her dreams as an author. Jackie had spent several years researching her family history and has used many of those finds as inspiration for her novels.

Printed in Great Britain
by Amazon